This book is dedicated to all the men and women who have put pen to paper to teach us about their era in history. Their words became our history books. . .and those books are the vehicles that transport us. . .to the year A.D. 29, when Jesus of Nazareth took His last steps to Calvary. . .or July 20, 1969, when Neil Armstrong and Edwin Aldrin took man's first steps on the moon. And, thanks to those same books, we can get to know people like Cleopatra, Abe Lincoln. . .even Moses!

Note to Readers

Yes, *Fire By Night* is a work of fiction, but the story is based on months of "time travel" made possible by—you guessed it—history books! When you turn this page, you will journey with me to Massachusetts, where Leah and Phillip Smythe and I will introduce you to the Boston of 1635 and 1636. The hurricane you'll read about actually happened, as did the building of what we now call Harvard University. You'll also learn about folks like Roger Williams and King Charles I. These men's deeds—good and bad—sparked events that resulted in this great nation of ours.

FIRE *by* NIGHT

Loree Lough

PUBLISHING, INC.

Uhrichsville, Ohio

© MCMXCVII by Barbour Publishing, Inc.

ISBN 1-57748-074-0

Published by Barbour Publishing, Inc.
P.O. Box 719
Uhrichsville, Ohio 44683
http://www.barbourbooks.com

ecpa Member of the
Evangelical Christian
Publishers Association

Printed in the United States of America.

Cover illustration by Chris Cocozza.
Inside illustrations by Adam Wallenta.

CHAPTER ONE

Weathering the Storm
Boston Harbor, 1635

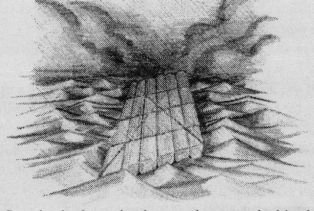

Phillip Smythe had survived several storms in his thirteen years. None of them had been this bad. The huge crashing waves had been driving him toward Boston's shore. But now, caught in a riptide, he was drifting farther and farther from the safety of Boston Harbor.

He lifted his head and squinted past the stinging raindrops that pelted his face. *If I can get a glimpse of Boston's harbor,* he thought, *perhaps I can steer the raft toward dry land.*

The raft was the only thing between Phillip and total destruction. To build it, he'd spent two days searching the stands of birch that grew deep in the forest. Phillip had needed fifteen straight and sturdy limbs, eight feet long and eight inches thick.

When he'd found them, it had taken another day to nail makeshift ladder rungs up the trunks of their trees. Once installed, he'd climbed the ladders and sawed off the big limbs.

After dragging each felled log to a clearing near the inlet, Phillip had placed them side by side and lashed them with a length of sturdy hemp. Next, he'd installed the all-important rudder. Last, he'd attached a makeshift sail.

In all, he'd invested a week in the raft's construction—an hour here, three hours there. It had been well worth every hard-won moment, every blister, every splinter.

"If a job's worth doing, it's worth doing well," his father had drummed into his head. *Now, there's a lesson I'm glad he taught me!* Phillip thought. *At least this raft is showing no signs of breaking apart in this storm.*

Still, Phillip gripped his lifeline tighter. He'd never felt closer to death's door. Not when he'd stood face-to-face with the fierce warrior on the woodland path. Not when he later met the same Indian in the bowels of a dark cave. Not even when he put his life on the line to defend White Wolf from murderous men.

Yes, he'd survived storms before. But this was no ordinary storm.

Phillip had noticed the ominous grey clouds overhead when he set sail at dawn. Something had told him to turn around. To make this trip another day. But then sister's ill health spurred him on. He decided to head out across the inlet to gather some of the scorpion wort that grew wild on Bristol Islc. According to his Narragansett friend, White Wolf, a strong tea brewed of the plant would calm her stomach. Then Leah could keep down the nourishing foods that she needed to eat if she were to get better.

Now, one cheek pressed hard against the rough bark deck of his raft, Phillip held his breath as yet another wave crashed over him. *It's a good thing you had the foresight to tie your supplies down before leaving Bristol Isle,* he told himself. *Otherwise, all your work would have been for—*

The craft suddenly rose fifteen or twenty feet on a hissing, spitting wave. Lightning exploded behind tattered grey clouds. A powerful thunderclap made his bones vibrate.

Good Lord Almighty, Phillip prayed, closing his eyes, *take me home. Please, God, see me through.*

The angry sea surged yet again, lifting him and his tiny boat high, higher, until he could see nothing but smoky sky all around him. The ropes that held his craft together creaked and groaned. He'd built his raft well, but was it strong enough to withstand a beating like this?

The watery world that surrounded him looked like a

monstrous, breathing being. It gurgled and growled as sea swells surged up like muscular arms. Waves curled like powerful fists and pounded down with the force and fury of a giant. If the Atlantic was Goliath, then Phillip was David. But Phillip had no weapon to use against the power of the sea.

If you'd heeded the sky's warning earlier, you wouldn't be here now, Phillip admitted. *You'd be home, safe and warm and dry.*

It had seemed such a short distance from Boston's shore to the other side of the inlet. Convinced it would take no more than an hour to make the trip to Bristol Isle and back, Phillip had decided to take the chance that he could beat the storm.

So much for outwitting nature! he scolded himself.

Now and then, the vicious storm calmed. Just for a moment, Phillip could catch a quick glimpse of the shore. Warehouses and stores along Boston's harborside streets peeked up from the horizon. Their roofs and chimneys reminded him of the hats that lined the shelves of the company store.

Before Geoffrey Martin and his parents had left town to follow Roger Williams, Phillip and his chubby friend had spent many hours pointing and chuckling at the ridiculous new cap styles some hatter in England had created from felt and flannel.

If I make it back in one piece, he promised himself, *I'll gladly buy one of those silly toppers, and wear it proudly 'round Boston!*

He'd heard of cyclones. Their swirling winds blew round and round 'til everything in their paths was sucked into their whirling centers. *Could this be a cyclone?* Phillip asked himself. He could only hope and pray that it was not. If there was any truth to the tales he and Geoffrey had over-heard sailors telling down by the wharf, he was doomed.

He remembered the way his mother always draped sheets over the windows to protect the well-oiled paper panes. She'd likely be standing in the doorway now, her shawl tied tightly around her shoulders, watching with worried eyes for him.

Would his father have hurried home from the carpentry shop to latch the gate and bolt the door? Would Leah have shooed the chickens into the henhouse so they'd be safe from windy blasts?

And what about Phillip's brother, John, and John's wife, Hannah? Had they seen the darkening skies in time to fasten their shutters so their little Zach would be spared the terror of witnessing the menacing gusts?

His sister Sarah's baby was due to be born soon. Was she inside her tidy cottage, safe and sound? And had her husband, Jake, who'd taught Phillip so much about his trade, returned home from his apothecary shop in time to protect his wife and unborn child from the cyclone's rage?

The beacon would have warned them if they'd seen it. Phillip lifted his head at the thought, hoping he was close enough to see the beacon that shone from the center of town.

"Thank You, God," he whispered. Burning pitch shone from the pot at the top of the tall pillar. It would continue to glow, bright and steady, at least for awhile.

Lying on his stomach, Phillip pressed his eyes against his

forearms and struggled to blink back hot tears. He'd turned thirteen on his last birthday, after all. He wasn't a boy any longer.

But the ugly truth was that he had no one but himself to blame for his predicament. If he'd paid attention to his instincts and stayed home, he wouldn't be riding the wild waves now. He had no choice but to lie still and wait it out—and hope the angry sea would soon tire of toying with him.

I'm cold, Phillip thought. *So very cold.*

He was tired, too. Tired of holding fast to the ropes that kept him from being eaten alive by the hungry waves. Tired of holding his breath as the waves pummeled him. He must have swallowed a gallon of the Atlantic's salty water, and his sickened stomach now churned like the swollen sea. He yawned, downing yet another mouthful of the briny liquid when he did.

You've got to stay awake! he commanded himself. *You don't want to end up at the bottom of the sea.*

If he was tired enough to yawn, he was tired enough to doze. And if he slept, even for a second, he was as good as dead.

He'd better have a plan, in case he did fall asleep.

Just then, he spied the end of the rope he'd used to lash the raft together. Flat on his stomach, he crept toward the craft's far corner. "Thank You, Lord!" he said, pulling the six feet of extra hemp from the water. "There's more than enough to tie myself to the deck." Wrapping the line tightly around his waist, he threaded it through several of the loops that held the birch logs together.

When he finished, he breathed a sigh of relief. Now, at least, he wouldn't be gobbled up by the hungry sea should fatigue overtake him.

It was a big mistake to look toward shore. Phillip's heart sank. The riptide had pushed him miles from shore.

Between the wind and the waves, you'll never make it back alive! His short trip across the inlet to gather the medicine would likely cost him his life. The storm had won.

But not yet! He'd accomplish one last good deed before breathing his last.

Phillip never went anywhere without his pencil, and he dug around for it now.

At first, he'd been fascinated by the writing tool. Ancient men, he'd learned in school, wrote with chunks of chalk and rock. Medieval monks, like the Egyptians before them, made their marks using metallic lead. *It was nothing short of a miracle,* Phillip thought, *that not so very long ago, someone had decided to encase graphite in wood to keep his hands clean while writing.*

All he needed now was something to write on. But what could there possibly be to use on this drenched raft? Suddenly, Phillip had an idea.

He'd built the raft of birch logs, but he hadn't peeled them. The rain and waves had caused the logs to swell and their bark to lift. Carefully, Phillip peeled a square of bark from one log.

"Please, Lord," he prayed, "let this work."

Dearest Mother and Father, he wrote, thanking God that his letters were adhering to the pulpy underside of the bark.

The plant in this bottle is known as scorpion wort. If you brew it into a tea, it will ease Leah's stomachache. I wish I could be there to see the results, but it seems I'm destined to meet my Maker this day, by way of this terrible cyclone. Think of me now and then, for I'll be thinking of you from my new home in heaven.
Your son,
Phillip W. Smythe

Carefully, Phillip rolled the bark like a scroll and slid it into the jar with the scorpion wort. Then he replaced its cork as tightly as his wet hands would permit. For a moment, he clutched the jar to his chest. God willing, the bottle, along with the message and the healing plant it held, would be carried to his family.

His family. . .

Oh, how he would miss them!

Phillip yawned again. *Remember,* he told himself, *the Bible says God's Kingdom is a paradise, where there is no suffering. At least you won't be cold anymore.*

Without another thought, he tossed the jar overboard. It bobbled and tumbled awhile before disappearing in the froth. "Carry it to shore, Lord," he prayed, "so that my death won't have been in vain."

CHAPTER TWO

Starting Over—Again

"Look. He's frowning."

"Well, it's no surprise. Don't forget—he was quite battered and bruised when we found him."

"Doc Turner says he probably swallowed gallons of sea-water."

"And that he might have broken a few bones."

"But we won't know for sure until he wakes up and tells us where it hurts."

"If he wakes up. . ."

Silence.

"I won't stand here and listen to such nonsense! He's going to be fine, just fine. You'll see!"

"Well, of course we all *hope* he'll be fine, but—"

"No 'buts' about it. We're praying, aren't we? So it's just a matter of time 'til he'll come around and. . ."

Phillip could make no sense of the discussion. He recognized the voices of his parents. He could also hear his older brother, John, and his little sister, Leah. There were other voices. He struggled to open his eyes. Who were they all so concerned about?

Warm tears fell on the back of his hand as a cool cloth was draped across his forehead. It felt good, but a sip of water would feel better.

I believe I could drain the whole rain barrel, he wanted to say. But he couldn't muster the strength to so much as lick his parched lips.

The discussion continued, distracting him for the moment from his thirst:

"He hasn't moved a muscle since we found him."

"And when the clock next chimes, a full day will have passed."

Who hasn't moved? Phillip wanted to know. But his head throbbed, and he still couldn't open his eyes.

"We mustn't lose hope. He's a strong boy."

"Stubborn, too. I say he'll be on his feet in no time."

Jake had said that, Phillip realized. He wanted to chuckle along with his brother-in-law, but couldn't. Suddenly, he was afraid. Try as he might, his body would not move.

I want to sit up! He tried to swallow, but his throat felt like sandpaper. *I want to know who this mysterious "he" you're talking about is, and I want a drink of fresh water!*

Water. . .

Acres and acres of it. The grey foaming water had pitched his tiny raft to and fro. It had happened in several blinks of an eye, it seemed. A gigantic wave had tossed Phillip, rolling him like his sister's rag doll, nearer, nearer the shoreline. Then it lifted him high, held him up for what seemed like forever, then hurtled him toward the earth in one merciless move.

Though he recalled hearing the sounds of snapping ropes and splintering wood—and his own terrified screams—Phillip did not remember hitting the ground. He only knew that the deafening racket, and his seemingly endless flight, ended as surely and as abruptly as the hard slamming of a door.

"I believe he's coming to."

"Oh, William. Do you think so?"

If only Phillip could put an end to the pain in his mother's worried voice.

"I've been praying and praying. God has answered my prayers!" Leah's sweet voice spoke near his ear.

Phillip summoned all his strength and opened his eyes. It

15

took a moment to focus, and when he did, he saw his whole family gathered round his bed.

Little Zach had crawled onto the foot of the bed. "Seeping?" the toddler asked, pointing a pudgy finger at his uncle.

"Yes," Hannah whispered, gathering her son into her arms. "Phillip is sleeping."

"Why does everyone look so serious?" Phillip croaked out. He was shocked by the raspiness of his voice.

Jake laid a hand on his shoulder. "Maybe it's because you were missing for a full day in the worst storm we've ever seen," his brother-in-law chuckled. "Then you decided to take a twenty-four-hour nap!"

Phillip managed a feeble grin. Then he frowned. "The scorpion wort. . . Did you find. . . ? Tea. . .for Leah. . ."

Mother glanced from her son-in-law to her ailing son and back again. "What on earth is he babbling about, Jake?"

"Ah, so *that's* what this was all about," he said, nodding. "White Wolf told Phillip about a plant that grows on Bristol Isle. Said a tea brewed from it would calm Leah's stomach and help her keep down the food that would build up her strength."

Mother perched on the edge of the bed and sandwiched Phillip's hands between her own. "Do you mean to tell me the raft. . .the trip across the bay. . ." She blinked, and a huge silvery tear rolled down her cheek. "All that was for Leah? You risked your life. . ."

Despite his pain and exhaustion, Phillip felt his cheeks blush. "Well, I started out on her behalf. But believe me," he added, aiming a half-grin at his little sister, "if I'd thought my

16

life was in danger. . ."

Leah giggled and kissed his cheek. "What a shame," she cooed sarcastically, "we never found your belongings, so it looks like you thumped your noggin for nothing."

He tried to hide his smile as he wiped her kiss from his cheek. "Not for nothing," he pointed out, "I discovered I could build a sturdy boat that'll take quite a beating. Though I'll admit, I never expected a storm like that!"

"None of us did," John said, scowling. "Who would have thought Boston could be flattened like a griddlecake in one afternoon!"

Phillip lifted himself onto one elbow. "Boston. . .flattened? Whatever do you mean?"

"I mean," John began, "that half the buildings in town have been destroyed, and most of those still standing are in such a shambles that they'll need to be torn down and rebuilt."

Phillip met Father's eyes. "The carpentry shop. . .?"

Father ran a work-hardened hand across his face and shrugged one shoulder. "Gone."

"And your tools?"

Father's shoulders slumped. "Gone, too. Like so much driftwood." Then, brightening slightly, he added, "George and I . . ." He swallowed hard, then continued. "George and I were planning some changes, anyway. The storm created the perfect opportunity to make them."

"The Lord works in mysterious ways," Hannah said, changing the subject.

"Amen," Mother agreed. "Now then, I imagine you're hungry. What can I get you to eat? I started a pot of mutton stew just this morning."

Phillip sank back onto the downy feather pillows and smiled. "Stew sounds wonderful," he said, pretending that his stomach wasn't upset. He patted his stomach and winced.

Mother was on her feet. "What is it, Phillip? Are you in pain? Tell me where it hurts."

"Shall I start at the top and work my way down, or the other way around?" he asked, grinning.

"That answer tells me he's just fine," Father said.

Mother left only long enough to fetch a bowl of stew. Phillip allowed her to spoon a bit of the stew into his mouth. "Broth only for you, until I'm sure you can keep it down," she said tenderly. She tore off a sop of crusty bread, swirled it in the bowl, and gently placed it in his mouth.

Phillip said nothing as she fluffed his pillows and folded the top edge of the crisp muslin sheet over the colorful patchwork quilt that covered him from shoulders to toes. He didn't wrinkle his nose when she pressed a maternal kiss to his cheek. Didn't roll his eyes when she lovingly brushed the hair from his forehead. It felt so good to be home that Phillip doubted he'd ever complain about her motherly ways again—even if she decided to perform them for all the boys in the school yard to see!

He took a deep breath, and gazed on the faces of those he loved.

But wait. Someone was missing.

"Where's Sarah?"

"Home," Jake announced. "With the baby." A grin lit his dark eyes.

"The baby! You mean. . . ."

"That's right," his brother-in-law said, puffing out his chest. "Your sister and I have a beautiful baby girl."

"A *big* baby girl," inserted Leah. "She's nearly twenty inches long already!"

"When was she born?"

"At almost the exact moment we found you on the beach," Jake said. "When I arrived home after seeing you safely tucked into your little bed," he added, winking, "your big sister was in her own bed. And a rosy bundle of energy was snuggled up beside her."

Mother clasped both hands in front of her. "The Lord saw fit to deliver my son from the stormy sea on one side of town while he delivered a ten-pound granddaughter on the other," she whispered. "Two miracles in one afternoon!"

"We were twice blessed," Father agreed.

Father awkwardly combed his thick, calloused fingers through Phillip's hair. Father's eyes told Phillip how much he was loved. And the slow, easy smile that lifted Father's mouth told Phillip that Father, too, knew he was loved.

George Sprague was buried on a dull, blustery summer day. He had died so another might live, Mother explained the morning after Phillip was rescued.

"According to what Melvin Talbot told your father, Mrs. Prentice said, 'I can't swim, and my boy's alone!' And you know Cousin George." She sighed, shaking her head.

"When he heard her cries, well, he just walked right out into the flooded street, intent on rescuing little Albert.

"The boy was perfectly safe on the steps of the grain shed, but he was bawling like a newborn lamb. And if I know George, it broke his heart to see the child in distress. He wasn't satisfied 'til he handed Albert over to his mother."

Mother paused and lowered her eyes. "It was as he returned to his own side of the street that. . ."

She cleared her throat before continuing. "I doubt he'd have done things differently, even if he'd known the flood waters would sweep him off his feet." She took a long, deep breath. "Such a waste. Such a sad, senseless waste."

Because the church had been one of the buildings destroyed by the cyclone, the pastor was forced to hold George's funeral in the small graveyard out back. Many of the headstones lay like wounded soldiers in the mud. The tidy fence that once surrounded the cemetery seemed to have been disassembled, board by white board.

Could it really have been just a year and a half ago, Phillip thought as he stood with the mourners, *that Cousin George's letter arrived in Plymouth, inviting Father to become his business partner?*

George had been like a brother to Phillip's father. He'd been an uncle to Phillip. Phillip couldn't imagine life without the big man's hearty laughter and playful winks. And he'd miss the conversations they'd had as George taught Phillip a better way to hold a hammer, turn a screw, plane a board.

Leah, still too weak from her bout with measles, had stayed home from the service. But John and Hannah and Sarah and Jake were there to comfort George's widow and son.

Even folks who were new to town came to pay their last respects to the bighearted carpenter. He had touched many lives, from the struggling young couple whose cart he'd repaired for free, to the one-legged man for whom he'd built a wheelchair.

George's wife, Catherine, stood in her plain black frock. Her left hand clutched the bow at the neck of her elbow-length cape. Blue eyes stared straight ahead.

And Thomas. . .

A rough sea breeze riffled his sandy-blond hair and reddened his pale, freckled cheeks. He seemed stunned by his father's death.

Death. It touched every life.

As the pallbearers lowered George's pine casket into the deep, rectangular hole, Phillip admitted that he was not ready in *any* way to deal with death. He looked at his father, his mother, his siblings and their children, and thanked God for each one.

CHAPTER THREE
Man of the House

Three weeks had passed since the storm struck. Just after breakfast, Father said to Phillip, "Son, come outside with me. There's something we need to discuss."

Phillip couldn't imagine what had painted the worried expression on Father's handsome face. He followed him to the end of their narrow walk and stood beside him near the gate.

"I'm sorry, Son," Father said, staring across the rutted road.

"Your dream of becoming an apothecary will have to wait. There's a ship in the harbor that'll be leaving for London at month's end, and I'm going to be on it."

"But. . .why?"

Father pressed his fingertips into tired eyes and sighed heavily. "I'm afraid there's no other way, Phillip. The king has asked the governor of our colony to send its best carpenters back to England to build furnishings for his palace. I have known for some time now that the governor wishes to include me in that group."

Father sighed again. "I've been putting off the decision, but it can't be delayed any longer. We need the money. It's as simple as that."

"But. . .but what about the shop?"

"The cyclone destroyed everything. What the winds didn't damage, the floodwaters carried away. There's not a respectable tool left. We haven't the funds to rebuild."

Phillip knew how true his father's words were. He'd helped dig through the mud and muck at the shop. Even after a week of sifting through the rubble, they'd found nothing worth saving except the chisel he'd left in the cave so long ago. "What will you build the king's furnishings with, since all your tools are gone?"

"According to the governor, the palace workshops will supply whatever tools I need."

"How long will you be gone?" Phillip asked.

"A year, possibly longer."

A year!

Father began to pace. "John's house was all but destroyed by the storm. They've tried to make do with what's left of it, but it's no use. Jake and Sarah and little Hope don't have room in their small cottage for three more people. So your mother and I have discussed it at length, and as we speak, he's packing his family's belongings. They'll be moving in here," he nodded toward their house, "by day's end."

Phillip shook his head. There was barely room for his parents, Leah, and himself. How would three *more* people fit in the tiny cottage?

"Since the workshop was leveled by the storm, John will have no means of making a living." Father cleared his throat. "So I've arranged for you and John to work for Sam Paulsen. He's the manager on the university project."

Phillip had heard all about the great college for men, scheduled to open its doors in the fall of 1636 in the center of town. According to all reports, construction would be funded by a grant from the General Court of the Massachusetts Bay Colony.

"There's plenty of work for good, strong men. I know Paulsen well. He'll treat you fairly and pay you well for an honest day's work."

Phillip was not afraid of hard work. What concerned him was that he'd barely served a year of his apothecary apprenticeship. Jake had explained early on that once begun, he must stick with his lessons. If an apprentice stopped studying for a year or more, he was required to start all over again.

In one short afternoon, the cyclone had all but leveled

Boston. It had destroyed his father's business and his brother's home. And it had killed Phillip's dream of becoming an apothecary just as surely as it had snuffed the life from Cousin George.

But this was not the time for self-pity. Right now, Father needed to know that when he left for London, the family would be well cared for.

"When are we to start work on the college?" Phillip asked.

"As early as week's end, if you're able."

Odd, Phillip thought to himself, *how such a calm morning has brought the end of my dreams.*

The days before Father's departure sped by too quickly. When they weren't helping Mother get Father's things ready for his trip, Phillip and Leah were busy helping John and Hannah get settled or were helping Sarah with her new baby. They were almost too busy to notice that the time had come for Father to leave.

Phillip and Leah said their good-byes at the breakfast table. Far easier to bid Father farewell in the privacy of his own home than to share his grief with the sailors who gathered at Boston Harbor.

Father's clothes were packed into his leather valise. After a hearty meal of potatoes and eggs, he unceremoniously jammed his wide-brimmed felt hat onto his head, shrugged into his short-waisted brown wool jacket, and headed for the door.

Phillip watched with quiet amazement as Father made no attempt to hide his tears. "I'll post a letter as soon as I'm able," he told Mother. Then he reached down and picked Leah up in a huge embrace.

"You keep on getting better," he said, huskily. "I'll be praying every day that my little Leah will be strong and well like the other girls when I come home."

Leah wrapped her arms around Father's neck. "I'll do everything I can to get strong," she promised. "I'll even drink those horrid teas Phillip keeps making for me."

Father kissed Leah on her pale cheek and swung her back to the floor. Then he turned to Mother, wrapped her in a warm hug, and kissed her long and hard. His voice was hoarse when he said, "I will miss you greatly, my love."

"And I you."

He looked over Mother's shoulder. "Phillip, won't you walk with me to the end of the road?"

Phillip stood a moment, unable to move after witnessing the loving farewell. Then he hurried to catch up with Father. "I'll do right by Mother and Leah, Father," he said, falling into step, "so don't you worry."

Father draped an arm across Phillip's shoulders. "I'll take many concerns with me on this journey, Phillip, but how my wife and daughter will be cared for is not one of them." He gave the boy a brusque, sideways hug. "I have complete faith in you."

At the end of the road, Father stopped. "What I'm about to say is not easy, son, and I'm trusting you to keep it to yourself."

Phillip met his father's grave expression with one of his

own. "Whatever you say is between us, I promise."

Father took a deep breath before continuing. "John is a good man, don't get me wrong, but he's. . .he's had some problems. Leaving his friends in Holland wasn't easy for him, and sometimes he does things he shouldn't do just to make people like him. He's not as strong or as levelheaded as you. He's going to need you to keep him on the straight and narrow."

Phillip's eyes widened. He'd never thought of his older brother as someone who needed his help.

"You'll attack your work at the college like a truc Smythe," Father continued. "You'll give Paulsen an honest day's work for your pay. John. . .may want to give up, and it'll be up to you to stoke his confidence."

Father met Phillip's eyes, shook his head, then focused on the pebbled path beneath his feet. "It's a heavy load to lay on your shoulders, you being the younger one and all, but I've always believed it's smarter to put the burden on the beast with the strength to carry it."

Father gave Phillip's shoulder an affectionate squeeze, then turned and headed down the road toward the harbor. "See that you get enough food and sleep, now," he called over his shoulder.

"I'll be fine," Phillip said, hoping his father had not heard the hitch in his voice. He cleared his throat, and said in strong, sure tones. "We'll *all* be fine. You'll see."

Father raised a hand and waved.

Cousin George's widow, Catherine, met Phillip on the path home. "I understand you'll be helping build the college in town," she said, her hands clasped primly at her waist.

He'd seen Catherine several times since the funeral. Each time, she'd looked so lost, so alone, that he went well out of his way to avoid her. What if he said some silly, thoughtless thing that brought back a painful memory? He'd given the matter a lot of thought as he tried to fall asleep each night, but no amount of consideration or prayer had provided the words that might comfort her.

"Quite a job for one so young," she said.

"Oh, it's not so bad," Phillip said. "Hard work makes the time pass quickly, and—"

Catherine rested her hand on Phillip's forearm. "Do you have any idea how much you resemble my dear George, Phillip?"

When at last he met her eyes, Phillip saw the hint of a smile flickering there. "I. . .I never really gave it much thought."

"You have his height—that much is for sure." She took her hand from his arm and pressed it against his cheek. "The same strong, broad jaw. You were blessed with his bighearted nature, too."

For a moment, Catherine bit her bottom lip, and then she continued. "I need to ask of you a favor, if you can spare me the time. . . ."

"I'd be happy to."

"It's Thomas," she said quickly, taking Phillip's arm and leading him down the path. "He's very confused, you know, by what happened to his father. He's. . .he's lonely, too, I'm afraid since his father. . .since George. . ."

Catherine took a breath and started again. "I was wondering

. . .if. . .maybe you could find a moment now and then to. . .to talk with Thomas. Perhaps when you're doing chores for your mother or running errands for Hannah. . . ." Her hands fluttered nervously as she chattered on. "I wouldn't ask you to interrupt anything important, naturally. . . . It's just that he has no one else, you see, and though I'm well aware that you're barely older than he, you've always seemed so much smarter and wiser and. . ."

Phillip shuffled along beside Cathcrine, scarcely hearing a word of what she said. *How much more will I be asked to bear?* he wondered. *John is older, and married, and a father, after all. Wouldn't he be a better choice for Thomas?*

Suddenly, Phillip found himself standing beside Catherine by the path to his house. "You are a wonderful, wonderful young man, Phillip Smythe," she said, patting his hand. "I am proud to have you in my family." She placed a damp kiss on his forehead. "You will be in my prayers," she added, and then she was gone.

Phillip stood for a moment, alone at the end of the walk, and tried to make sense of it all. Why had the adults in his life—his parents, John and Hannah, Sarah, and now Catherine—started treating him like some wise old man?

Phillip scrubbed both hands over his face and shook his head. "Lord," he muttered under his breath, "I'm sure You have some plan for me in all this." As he walked up the path toward the front door, he added, "But it sure would be a lot easier if You'd let me in on it."

CHAPTER FOUR
Fire!

A few weeks after Father left, Phillip was beginning to think that life had settled into its new routine. The house was crowded with the addition of John and his family, but Mother appreciated the extra help from Hannah. Leah seemed to be getting stronger every day.

The only cloud on Phillip's horizon was John's puzzling behavior. Since Father had left, John seemed to spend more time away from home. He'd made some new friends, and

Phillip didn't trust them at all. What's more, John's work was slipping, and Phillip found himself covering for his brother at their job.

Waking up before dawn one day, Phillip felt groggier than usual. He rubbed his eyes as he reached for his clothes. Suddenly his eyes opened wide. He could do little more than stare, horror-struck, at the sight before him. Raging flames burned so bright and hot, they lit up the Smythe house like the summer sun. Sooty grey smoke hovered near the ceiling and filled the house with choking clouds.

His world was on fire!

What about Mother, Leah, John and Hannah, and little Zach? Phillip had to warn them! Throwing on his clothes, Phillip hollered at the top of his lungs. He stuffed his feet in his shoes and scrambled down the loft ladder, still yelling, "Mother! John! Fire!"

"Fi-wup," called a small voice from across the room. "Fi-wup, what smells?"

"Zach," Leah said, grasping his tiny hand, "stay here with me." Then, in a voice as thick and crackling as the blaze, she added, "Phillip, I can barely breathe. We need to get everyone out of here."

He searched for a napkin, an apron, anything to protect their faces, and grabbed his mother's snood from her bedpost. "Hold that over your face!" he ordered. "Stay low to the floor and get yourself and Zach out of here. Go to Catherine's and wait until Mother, Hannah, and I get there."

Leah nodded her understanding and scooped Zach into her

arms. She ran with him out the front door, choking on the smoke.

Phillip peered through the smoke-filled rooms, trying to find Mother. A figure across the room darted perilously toward the inferno, only to fling a useless dipper of water onto the hot, hungry flames. Mother!

Phillip ran to her. "Mother, we must leave before we burn up with the house!" he cried.

"You go on," she said. "I have to get this fire under control."

"It's no use, Mother," he hollered over her shoulder. "It's already out of control. We *have* to get out of here." Grabbing her arm, he hurried her toward the door.

Hannah, who'd been calling for her husband since the chaos began, grabbed Phillip's arm. "I can't find John," she gasped. "Have you seen him?"

"No, I have not," he choked out, leading both Hannah and Mother to the safety of the yard. "See to Mother, and I'll find him."

"Oh, Phillip!" Hannah cried. "What if you can't find him? What if something has happened to him!"

Phillip ran sooty hands through his hair and grimaced. "He's fine, Hannah. I'd stake my life on it." He swallowed hard and took a deep breath to summon patience. "You'll find Zach with Leah at Catherine's," he growled. "Get over there, now! There's not a minute to lose."

Hannah grasped her mother-in-law's hand, but Mother yanked her arm free. "I'm not going anywhere," she said quietly. "This is my home, and I'll not leave it!"

"Mother, your hair is singed and your lips are blistered." Gently, Phillip wrapped his arm around her shoulders. "What more are you willing to risk on this pile of sticks and stones?"

Absently, she ran a hand through her hair and stared at him, as if trying to understand the words.

"Go to Zach," Phillip said to Hannah. "I'll take care of— Mother, stop!"

Mother had run from them and was headed straight back into the burning house. Phillip bounded after her.

The fire gnawed through the roof like a ravenous beast, and its powerful draft lifted his mother's prized lace tablecloth toward the gaping hole. It fluttered like a wind-billowed sail as she clutched the air to save it. Sparks filled the air like the golden stars of a fairy's wand, mesmerizing mother and son with their dazzling brilliance. The delicate ivory cloth burst into flame, shriveled, and vaporized in the withering heat.

In one swift move, Phillip whisked the shawl from around Mother's shoulders, drenched it in the water bowl, and flung it over her. In the next, he pinned her arms to her sides, slung her over his shoulder, and raced for the door. The fiery beast was on his heels now, its gaping jaws spread wide, roaring its malevolent intent. He could smell the putrid scent of burning leather.

His boots were on fire!

Clothes, shoes, Mother, and all, Phillip leapt into the water trough in the center of the street.

For an instant, fire and liquid were at war.

He heard the sizzle and hiss of the water's victory. But the liquid had won more than one battle. The cold dunk broke

Mother's panic. Sitting up in the trough, she pushed back her hair with trembling fingertips and took a deep, shuddering breath.

In shock himself, and groping for words, Phillip could think of nothing to say. "I'm. . .I'm sorry about your tablecloth, Mother."

She blinked. Frowned. Then she grinned at the absurdity of the untimely comment. Oblivious to the gathering onlookers who'd been awakened by the fire's stench and heat, she began to laugh.

After all they'd just been through, that laughter was music to Phillip's ears. Mother and son fell weakly into one another's arms, shaking with manic glee that lasted a minute or more. Gradually, as their laughter abated, they rose, dripping, from the trough.

"Well," Mother sighed, stepping from the trough, "the house is gone, but we're not."

Phillip shook his head. "You'll never believe this, but I'm famished."

Grinning slightly, Mother replied, "I'll get the vittles, if you'll start the fire."

The laughter started up again, and then, as if in answer to a prayer, the skies opened up and a steady rain began to fall.

Phillip dropped to his knees and folded his hands. "Oh, Lord," he said, "thank You for delivering us from the evil of this fire."

The soothing sound of his words blended with the pattering of raindrops on the hard ground. Mother knelt beside him and began a silent prayer of her own. With every word that passed her lips, the fire burned with less fury.

Mother lifted Phillip's chin with the tip of her forefinger and stared deep into his eyes. Then, ever so lightly, she kissed his cheek. "God has been thanked. Now thank *you*, Phillip, for saving my life and for reminding me that all is not lost. Go to Catherine's, now, and get some breakfast. I'll be along shortly." She rose then, and drew him to his feet.

"If you're staying, I'm staying," Phillip declared. "I'll not leave you alone."

Mother sighed deeply, then glanced at her ruined house. Shaking her head, she smiled in resignation. "You are more than a son, Phillip William Smythe. You are a true friend."

Taking a last lingering look at what had been their home, she turned her back and took Phillip's hand. "All right, then, we'll go to Catherine's together."

"It's no use, Mrs. Smythe," called Andy Porter, one of the men who had started a bucket brigade. "We've got the fire out, but there's no saving anything that was in the house."

"My family thanks you for trying," Mother said. "At least the rain kept the fire from spreading to other homes." To the rest of the men who huddled nearby, pails in hand, she added, "Go on back to your wives and children now, for a long, hard day awaits you."

"If there's anything we can do. . ."

"Thank you, but we'll be just fine, Mr. Porter."

"These cottages go up like that," he said, snapping his fingers. "Tinder is what they are. Tinder boxes!" he repeated.

"It's a wonder more houses don't burn in the dead of night."

Once he'd disappeared into the crowd, Mother took Phillip's hand once more. "Why did you stay, Phillip? Why didn't you go with Hannah and the others?"

"I couldn't leave you, Mother."

"But where was John? He's the oldest. By rights, *he* should have been here."

Phillip didn't have the heart to tell his mother about the rumors he'd been hearing for weeks. John just wasn't the same. First he'd picked up those bad friends. Then he'd started to smell like he'd been drinking. Now men Phillip worked with were talking about the way John had been betting with the sailors at the harbor, betting—and losing. Learning about these rumors, on top of losing Cousin George, on top of having Father thousands of miles across the sea, on top of the destruction of her home might break Mother's heart.

"I imagine John went in search of water. It all happened so fast, I don't suppose he had time to get back and help," Phillip suggested. Almost as an afterthought, he put in, "John is probably the reason the neighbors came as quickly as they did."

Mother closed her eyes and sighed. "It's a lovely story." She met Phillip's eyes to say, "Pity it isn't true, isn't it?"

The pain in her eyes was almost too much to bear. *How much does she know?* Phillip wondered. *Could someone have told her what John's been up to these past weeks?* He shrugged. "Accidents happen, that's all. Things got out of hand too fast for him to *be* any help. I'm sure he'd have been here if—"

"As it turns out, John's help wasn't needed." Mother stopped in her tracks and, despite the rain that pelted down, simply looked at Phillip with pride. Her smile faded as she brought a soggy and soot-smeared wad of parchment from her apron pocket. "There was a knock at the door just before the fire. When I opened it, I found this."

Pursing her lips, she handed the folded note to Phillip. "I've made up my mind not to speak of this to anyone. But you deserve to know the truth."

Brow furrowed with puzzlement, he smoothed the paper and read the ink-blurred words aloud: "John William Smythe now knows the price for reneging on his debts."

Phillip clenched his jaw and crumpled the parchment in his hands. "What will he destroy next?" His heart thundered with fury. He looked from his mother's worried face to the scrap of paper clutched in his hand. "They knew his family was inside, and still they did this? To frighten him into paying his gambling debts? It makes no sense. *John* is the one who owes them money. Why take it out on—"

Mother retrieved the threatening message and jammed it back into her pocket. "Don't try to make sense of deeds done by a gang of ne'er-do-wells. You'll only muddle your mind."

Phillip hid his face in his hands. "I'm sorry. I should have told you the moment I first heard the rumors. Perhaps if I had, we could have done something. I didn't want to worry you. I hoped the rumors weren't true, and that if they were, that John would set himself straight."

Unexpectedly, Mother tugged his hands away from his face and stroked his rain-soaked hair. "What your brother has been

37

doing is no more your fault than what happened here this morning," she assured him. Her gaze traveled to the ruins of their home.

Phillip opened his mouth to protest, but her raised hand silenced him. "If you bear any blame, I bear it, too." she said.

He quirked a brow. *"You!* I don't understand."

"I've suspected what's been going on for some time now. I knew your brother had fallen in with a bad lot and that he was doing bad things simply to win their friendship. I did nothing to stop it, because, truthfully, I didn't know *how* to stop it."

"Have they threatened him before?"

"Yes," she nodded, "several times. Nothing as blatant as this, of course." Mother glanced back at the house. Smoke still puffed stubbornly above glowing embers that coated the rush-covered cottage floor.

Phillip wondered, *What sort of havoc would the misfits down at the harbor wreak next?*

CHAPTER FIVE

The Fight

Most of the time, Phillip was glad to have the job building the college, for it kept his mind occupied. From dawn to dusk, as he measured and hammered and sawed—using tools provided by the General Court—he didn't have to think about anything else. Not the fact that Cousin George was gone forever. Not that

Father was so far from home. Not that the cyclone's flood-waters had destroyed the family business and that Sarah wasn't recovering her health after the birth of little Hope. Not that John was letting the entire family down.

Once he left the construction site, however, life took a different twist. The moment he arrived home, Catherine or Hannah or his mother had a lengthy list of chores for him to do, and while the women prepared supper, Phillip would chop and gather wood, check his snares and set them anew, and fetch buckets of water needed for cooking and cleaning. When at last he fell into bed each night, the boy was so exhausted that he immediately dropped to sleep.

The one bright spot in his life was Leah. Regular doses of the herbs White Wolf had taught Phillip about had restored strength to Leah's body. Phillip doubted Father would recognize the energetic, bubbly girl who now bustled around their home. Phillip hardly recognized her himself. She spent much of her time at Jake and Sarah's house, taking care of baby Hope so that Sarah could rest.

One afternoon as he walked the mile and a half home from his job, Phillip thought of White Wolf. He hadn't seen his Narragansett friend in months and wondered how his friend was faring. He thought of Geoffrey, too, and pondered what the boy might be up to in Salem. Surely Mr. Martin had not required *his* son to set his dreams aside to take over all the responsibilities that went hand-in-hand with being the man of the family.

Phillip quickly suppressed his bitter thoughts. Self-pity could lead a man into waters even more treacherous than those he'd survived during the cyclone. He would do right by his father without complaint—just as his father had done right by his grandfather. Besides, if God had heard Phillip's prayers, Father would be returning on the next ship that dropped anchor in the harbor. And according to Old Bertram, who piloted the skiff that carried people, livestock, and dry goods from ship to shore, the next vessel was due to arrive within the week.

The family hadn't received any word from Father. Every morning since his father's hasty departure, Phillip prayed that Father was happy and healthy and being treated fairly by his new employer, King Charles I.

Soon, he hoped, his father would return with a stipend in his pocket. The money would be more than enough to rebuild their home and the shop as well. They could return to business as usual, and John's behavior would become Father's problem once again. The only thing left to pray for was that the Atlantic would not rise up and interfere with his dreams!

It was crowded in Cousin Catherine's little house. Though it was larger than the Smythe cottage had been, the Sprague's residence had been built for a family of four or five—not one of eight!

At night, Thomas, Leah, and baby Zach were stacked like kindling beside Hannah and Catherine on the only two featherbed mattresses in the house. On those rare nights when John was home, he dozed on the sofa Father had built for Catherine. Mother slept upright in the hard wooden rocker near the fireplace, with a warm shawl around her shoulders, and Phillip snoozed on a crude cob-stuffed pallet on the floor at her feet.

Phillip did his best to help his cousin Thomas. As Catherine had pointed out, Thomas had changed since his father's death. Instead of being outgoing and friendly, Thomas was subdued and quiet. Even Leah rarely succeeded in getting her cousin to laugh.

But as the weeks passed, Thomas relaxed under Leah's gentle teasing. And as they did chores together, Phillip told Thomas how he felt about Father's absence. Soon, Thomas began talking with Phillip about his own pain at his father's death. In time, Thomas found a proper place in his heart to put his father's death. . .and his memory. Little by little, his boisterous behavior returned.

Things were going smoothly until the afternoon when John came upon the boys as they gathered wood for the cook fire. "What are you up to?" he demanded.

"Why, we're robbing the Bay Colony at musket point, of course," Phillip sneered. Under normal circumstances, he would not have been so sarcastic, but John had become more of a problem than Father had feared, and Phillip was tired of dealing with him.

"No need to mock me, stinkpot. I was only asking a simple question."

"There's nothing simple about you these days," Phillip retorted, not even trying to hide his annoyance. "You're a lazy, good-for-nothing. Your wife and son would starve to death if it weren't for me doing your share of work at the college.

You're away from the site more often than you're there. I'm fed up with doing your job and mine, too."

"So quit, then! Who asked you to be my protector?"

Father did! Phillip wanted to shout. But he'd promised to keep Father's secret. "Tell me this, big brother," he said in a soft, deliberately controlled voice. "If I don't shoulder your responsibilities, who will feed and clothe your family?"

John snickered. "We're living in Catherine's house, eating the food our own mother prepares. My dear wife does more than her share of woman's work, so what have you to complain about, stinkpot?"

John laughed, long and loud. "What! You don't like my little nickname for you anymore. . .*stinkpot?*"

Narrowing his eyes, Phillip rasped, "No. . .I don't like it. Not one bit."

What happened to the brother who counseled me when Father's scoldings broke my spirit, or some schoolmate's offhanded remarks hurt my feelings? Phillip wondered. He missed the John he had grown up with. Missed the John his brother had been before gambling and ale had changed him. Didn't he feel the least bit guilty that his habits had cost his family their home? Was there no remorse in his soul for the sins he'd committed—sins that cost his mother and sister, his wife and his son dearly?

"I know what you're thinking," John spat. "You're up on that pedestal of yours, looking down at me, judging me."

" 'Judge not that ye be not judged,' " Thomas injected.

"When I want a Bible verse recited, I'll chose the time and

43

the place. . .and the verse!"

Thomas shrugged. "It could have been. . .*verse,*" he said, grinning slyly.

It wasn't much of a joke, so Phillip didn't understand why it raised John's hackles. The older Smythe doubled up both fists and stumbled toward Thomas like a wild pig, grunting and growling as he went. "Since your father's gone, you need a man to beat some sense into your head from time to time, and I'm just the man to do it!"

Thomas's eyes widened and bulged with fear as John advanced upon him. "He's mad, Phillip," he said, cowering beside his cousin. "The drink and the gambling have rotted his brain!"

Phillip closed the short gap that had separated him from John. "You don't want to fight with me, instead, do you?"

Without warning, one of John's fists smashed into Phillip's face, sending him reeling. He sat there on the ground—stunned as much by the fact that John had hit him as by the pain of the blow itself. He winced as he worked his aching jaw back and forth. He'd seen his share of fistfights, but Phillip had never participated in one. He was amazed at how much a sock to the head could hurt!

"Get up, stinkpot," John hissed, fists raised for combat now. "You think you're such a big man. Let's see you fight like one!"

Phillip rose to the challenge and faced his brother, toe to toe. "I may not be a man yet," he countered, "but when I become one, I won't get drunk and pick fights with boys!"

"Drunk! Who, me?" John's eyes widened in surprise. "Why, I'm not drunk, you little—"

"I can smell you from here," Phillip interrupted. "There's likely a gallon of ale swirling in your gut right now."

John threw another punch, but Phillip blocked it with a raised forearm. "See what drink does to a man, Thomas?" Phillip shouted. "Makes you blind to your own ugliness. Puts you so low, you'd beat your own flesh and blood for sport!"

This time when John jabbed, Phillip bobbed right, neatly avoiding the blow.

With the force of a cannonball, John exploded forward, grabbed Phillip by the hair of his head, and wrenched him to the ground. Before Phillip could respond, John landed on top of him, his knees pinning Phillip's arms against his sides.

What followed seemed like a blur to Phillip's unbelieving eyes. John's blows came hard and fast, each landing with a sickening crack on his quickly swelling face.

"You're nothing but a big bully," Thomas yelled. "What would your father say if he could see you now?"

The question stopped John cold. His fists hovered threateningly in midair, and he turned his baleful stare toward Thomas.

Concern for his cousin triumphed over fear, and Thomas continued his angry tirade: "*My* father thought you hung the moon. But he was wrong! You. . .you ought to. . ." Frustrated, he searched his mind for an appropriate insult. "You ought to be hung at noon!" Despite his fear, a small grin curved the corners of his mouth at the cleverness of his rhyme.

The words hit John harder than any of the thumps he'd landed on Phillip's face. The anger slowly drained from his face, supplanted by shame as he raised himself to one knee. He extended a hand to help Phillip up, but the boy, his battered face hidden behind a crooked forearm, never saw it. John's guilt grew as he stood and shuffled woodenly toward the path that would lead him home, muttering under his breath as he went.

Thomas knelt beside Phillip, wincing when his cousin exposed his bloodied face. "Why didn't you fight back?" he asked as he helped his cousin sit up.

Phillip snatched back his hand. "Because I didn't, that's all," he snapped.

"But you would only have been defending yourself."

How could he explain to a boy younger than himself what *he* didn't understand? He needed time to sort out what had just happened. . .what had *been* happening for months, now.

"Take the firewood to your mother," he growled, stooping to pick up the kindling he'd dropped. "I'll be along shortly."

He was glad that Thomas didn't badger him with the usual barrage of questions. Phillip waited until his cousin was out of sight before stepping onto the well-trod trail. He'd gone about halfway home when he encountered Jake going the other way.

"What's happened to your face, lad!" Jake exclaimed. "You look like you've been chewed up and spit out by an angry dragon!"

Phillip felt the heat of shame color his cheeks. "I tripped. That's all." If the lie worked on the Irishman, it was sure to work on his mother.

Jake stared hard at the boy. "Do I look to you like a man born yesterday, Phil? To get mangled like that, you'd need to start your fall from the top of the tallest tree!" He stood in front of the boy, blocking his path. "Now. Tell me what *really* happened."

Phillip took a deep breath. "Well, John—"

"Your *brother* did this to you? What sort of madman would do such a thing to his own flesh and blood!"

Phillip stared at the hard ground.

"He was drunk again, wasn't he?"

The boy's silence was Jake's answer.

"I saw him not five minutes ago. He didn't look to me like a man who'd been in a fight."

Phillip's flush deepened. "That's because I didn't fight back," he said in a small, soft voice.

For a long moment, Jake studied his young brother-in-law's face. "And I suppose you're feeling a mite embarrassed about that, are you?"

The boy nodded.

"Your father's a good and decent man, Phillip, and I'll wager he taught you what my own pa taught me. You can't win a fight with a drunkard."

Father had indeed taught that lesson to his youngest son. Still, Phillip couldn't help worrying that John would return to dish out more of the same.

"No need to fret about it, lad. Why, he was so far gone, it's not likely he'll remember what happened when he sobers up in a few hours."

"Oh, I think he'll remember, all right, and I think he intends to make me sorry I let him best me."

Jake met the boy's eyes. "Is that what you think? Do you really believe John bested you? If either of you won that ridiculous battle," Jake said, one brow raised and a finger aimed at Phillip, "it was you. Because you chose not to stoop to his level."

"But—"

Jake drew a deep breath. "You don't understand right now. I realize that. But someday, when you're full grown, this will make complete sense to you. Mark my words." Then, glancing in the direction John had gone, he muttered, "Why, I've a good mind to. . ."

The horrible expression that had darkened his brother's face had terrified Phillip, and the beating he'd doled out had scared him, too. But now he had a whole new reason to be afraid. "You won't. . .you wouldn't tell Mother, would you?"

"You may as well dance to the fiddler's tune right off, lad, 'cause she's going to find out sooner or later anyway."

He jammed his fists into his pockets and scowled. "Then let it be later. I promised Father I'd take care of things." He tucked in one corner of his swollen mouth, wincing with pain when he did. "Does *this* look like I'm taking care of things!" he bellowed, pointing at his abused face.

Jake gave him a rough, sideways hug. "It looks to me like you're doing a fine job taking care of things. Your problem is that you take *too* much care." After another hug, he added, "Calm yourself, lad. It'll do no good to get riled up now. You know as well as I do that your ma deserves to hear what happened. But I won't be the one who tells her, if that's what you want."

Phillip expelled an exasperated sigh. "It's just that I promised Father I'd look after my mother and my sister and Thomas and his mother." He lowered his head. "I aim to do it, too." He met his brother-in-law's eyes, his gaze challenging the man to a silent oath of allegiance. "So if you have any affection for me at all, you'll keep your mouth shut."

Jake shook his head. "I do, and I will." They walked a bit in silence before he added, "Now, let's take a hike down to the river and get you cleaned up a bit. . .else your mother will take one look at that face and think you've brought raw meat home for dinner!"

"Are you worried she'll invite me to hop into the stewpot when she sees me?" Phillip asked, grinning crookedly.

Jake's smile never reached his eyes. "Don't know about that," he said under his breath, "but one thing's sure: *Somebody's* going to be in hot water this night!"

Chapter Six

The Secret Project

"Phillip," Thomas gasped, bending at the waist and leaning palms on knees as he stopped in the clearing in the forest. "I've been looking everywhere for you."

Phillip laid down the hammer and regarded his cousin carefully. "There are very few places I'd be these days," he said dully, counting on the fingers of one hand. "Working at the college, working at your mother's house, or working here."

With the back of his hand, Thomas wiped perspiration from

his brow. "Leah said you'd mentioned something about visiting Jake this morning, so I started my search for you at the apothecary shop."

At the mere mention of his elusive dream, Phillip winced. "I only stopped in to see if I might trade Jake a few chores for a few grams of scorpion wort for Leah's stomach distress."

While Thomas chattered on about the events of his day, Phillip's mind wandered. At the age of thirteen—just one short year ago—he'd considered it a terrible inconvenience to set aside a puzzle or a game in answer to his father's stern, "Phillip, have you checked your snares?" The twice-daily duty of gathering of wood seemed an onerous, backbreaking chore. Why, even a simple request from his mother, like, "Phillip, will you mind the stewpot?" had seemed a great, burdensome activity.

Now, at fourteen, the responsibilities of a man had been unceremoniously thrust upon him. People depended upon him for so many things.

How could life change so much in such a short time? he asked himself. Phillip sighed.

Thomas's high-pitched, agitated voice broke through Phillip's thoughts. "And *now* she wants *me* to pluck the chickens!" the boy was saying, "and I haven't a clue how to do it. Will you teach me, Phillip?"

Phillip bit back his annoyance. He picked up the hammer from where he'd placed it on the worktable when Thomas arrived and resumed banging on the stubby, triangular-shaped nail that would hold two boards together. "And where would

I find time to teach you to pluck a chicken?" he asked between hammer blows. "Why, I barely manage to find time to swallow a few bites of food each day!"

Thomas merely stared at him. "Whenever *my* face got all screwed up like that, my father would say, 'Your face is going to stay that way!' " Playfully, he nudged his cousin. "Keep out of the cemetery," the boy added, narrowing his eyes. "That's my advice to you."

"Whatever are you babbling about, Thomas?"

"Well. . .with that scowl on your face these days, folks might mistake you for a statue and stand you in the ground to watch over some deceased family member!"

His cousin's statement, Phillip knew, had been intended to coax a smile. Instead, it riled him further. Using the hammer's handle as a pointer, he captured Thomas's attention. "Do you know who taught *me* to pluck a chicken?"

Thomas shook his head.

"You're looking at him! I learned by watching my mother and yours." He couldn't help a slight grin of pride. "Added a few tactics and techniques of my own that make the process more efficient," he said, remembering when his mother and sister had had the measles and he'd killed—then *skinned* rather than plucked—a fat red hen.

"I've watched them. And to tell the truth," Thomas admitted, wrinkling his nose, "I don't *want* to learn how."

Phillip could only sigh in resignation. "Thomas," he began, stacking two more chunks of wood onto the worktable, "if you're ever asked to do something you *want* to do, I hope you'll come find me, because I'd hate to miss such a history-making event.

"Why were you looking for me, anyway?" he asked, changing the subject. "You didn't come all this way just to ask me how to pluck a chicken."

Immediately, Thomas brightened as he remembered why he'd searched Phillip out. "There's a ship on the horizon. Old Bertram says it set sail in London, and that means your father will likely be on it!"

Bert had explained the basic ship scheduling procedures the day Father left for England. An Atlantic crossing could last from three to six months, depending upon the weather. His father had been gone nearly *fourteen* months. Depending on the weather and the amount of work he had to do, Father might be on this ship.

Phillip's foul mood evaporated instantly. "How far out to sea is she? A day's sail? Two?"

Thomas shrugged. "She's not at sea. A messenger from Plymouth said she's dropped anchor there already. And since it's no more than a hard day's ride away, she ought to arrive here in a few days, at most. She's little more than a dot on the horizon now, but there's a good wind blowing. I don't expect it'll be long."

It was the best news Phillip had heard in ages! The horrible events of the past several months—the storm and all its destruction, Cousin George's untimely death, his father's absence, the fire that leveled his house—fled his mind. Phillip grabbed Thomas by the shoulders and gave him a brotherly

53

shake. "Let's head over to the harbor and see if we can calculate when she'll drop anchor."

"But what about your work?" Thomas asked, nodding toward the temporary woodworking shop Phillip had created in the middle of the forest.

He refused to let the reminder of all he had yet to accomplish dampen his mood. "See that pile of scrap wood there?" he directed, releasing the boy's shoulders.

Thomas nodded. "They're the boards we found in town after the cyclone."

"That's right." He launched into a brief explanation of how he intended to use them.

Thomas's brows drew together in the center of his forehead. "You're building *what?*"

"Forms."

"What kind of forms?"

"To make bricks."

"You don't know how to make bricks." He punctuated his statement with a sarcastic chuckle.

Phillip ignored Thomas's mockery, his lips forming a thin line. Thomas's reaction was precisely the reason he hadn't told a soul the *real* reason he'd been working deep in the woods late at night.

He'd satisfied his suspicious mother with a hasty response to her questions regarding his mysterious late-night trips to the woods. He'd never told an outright lie to either of his parents, and certainly hadn't wanted to start then, but when his mother pressed him for the truth, his response seemed to alleviate her concerns: "I go there to be alone, to think," he'd said, "and to pray for the strength to keep doing what I must until Father returns."

And the answer was true, after all. Not an hour passed as Phillip worked that he didn't thank God for the hard-found solitude that was so elusive in Catherine's crowded house. Often, he pleaded with his heavenly Father to instill in him the strength to press on. If he had a shilling for every time he'd asked the Almighty to help him locate the ingredient most necessary to make it all possible. . .

His mother wouldn't have known about the late-night work at all, if it hadn't been for Leah. Unbeknownst to Phillip, she'd followed him to the forest one moonlit night. He might never have known his sister had trailed along if she hadn't fallen asleep standing against a tree, and landed with a loud *thump* in the underbrush beside the woodland path!

"What are you doing out here!" Phillip had demanded, helping her up.

Checking to make sure she hadn't skinned an elbow in the fall, Leah had said, "I wanted to see for myself where you go every night."

"If you'd been asleep, as you were supposed to be, you'd never have known I was gone in the first place!"

Leah's laughter echoed through the air. "Sleep! Amid all the racket you make, getting up to sneak out of the house! You're joking, right?"

He'd ignored Leah's chiding. "I spend time in the woods to get a little peace and quiet. I can't have a minute to myself with seven other people prowling around me, now can I! So I come here for my privacy and solitude." This, too, was true, for as he worked, Phillip often thanked God for the peace and quiet that shrouded this place.

But his answer had not convinced Leah. "You don't really think working, when you should be sleeping, will clear your head, do you?"

Phillip dusted off the pine needles and dried leaves that had stuck to Leah's dress when she fell. "I know it seems strange, but it works," he'd said, shrugging.

Leah had stood there, silently regarding him through narrowed eyes. And then she'd said, "These have been trying times, haven't they?"

Phillip gave no response.

"Hannah is worried about you. I heard them talking. They said you've been looking tired and drawn, and working harder than a fourteen-year-old should. You don't want to end up being sick like I was for so long, do you?"

Phillip grumbled, "If you don't get your sleep, you'll be back to spending your days in bed."

"That's a thought," Leah had chuckled. "Then I wouldn't have to take care of the chickens, and you'd get to do more cooking again!"

Leah had wrapped her arm around her brother and given him a big squeeze. Then they'd both crept back home. They hadn't spoken of their conversation, nor had Leah followed him into the woods ever again.

Phillip had regained his privacy. Until tonight.

Phillip's long silence seemed to bring Thomas around. His cousin held up his hands in mock surrender. "All right, all right! So you *do* know how to make bricks. I'm sorry for doubting you."

Phillip stared at the boy, grinning as he narrowed his eyes. "Don't be sorry, be helpful. The sooner we get this job done, the sooner we'll be at the harbor." Nodding at the lumber, he said, "Now hand me a board. And after we've plotted that ship's course, I'll show you the best way to ready a chicken for the pot!"

In all his fourteen years, only two letters had been addressed to Phillip Smythe.

The first had come from Salem, and had been written by Geoffrey Martin, the chubby, freckle-faced redheaded boy who had welcomed Phillip to Boston. In no time, the boys had become fast friends. And it seemed that in no time, Geoffrey had left. In his letter, Geoffrey described Salem, the city where Roger Williams had led his followers. It sounded like a bustling, fascinating place. But between the lines, Phillip read Geoffrey's feelings of isolation and fear. He understood those emotions well, for he'd felt the same way when his own father had moved the family from Plymouth to Boston.

Phillip stared at this, his second-ever letter.

Delivered in a crisp envelope from the ship Phillip had prayed would carry his father home, the letter bore the great seal of the house of King Charles I. Any excitement that might have been generated at the sight of the fanciful *C,* pressed into a thick bed of beeswax dyed red with iron oxide, fizzled even before it formed.

The letter had come instead of Father, and nothing written on any parchment page could take Father's place.

Phillip held the single parchment page in trembling hands, unable to focus on the bold black ink that swirled across the page in thirteen tidy lines. It didn't matter that his tears of regret blurred the words, for he'd read them so many times, he could have recited them by heart.

At the top of the page, his father had written "The tenth day of February, in the Year of Our Lord, One Thousand Six Hundred and Thirty-Six."

This was August fourth—a full six months since the letter had been written. It had been *fourteen* long months since Father had left home. Phillip took a deep breath and read his letter to the family members gathered around Cousin Catherine's table:

Dear Phillip,

I regret that I will not be aboard the next Boston-bound ship. The king has commissioned another suite of furnishings. Though he did not state his request as an outright order, I feel I should not refuse him, for if we're to rebuild when I return, every shilling will count.

I trust you are taking care of your mother and sister, and watching over Catherine and Thomas. I think of only one other more often than you, my son, and your sisters and brother. (And you are not surprised that the

other is your dear, sweet mother, now are you?)
 If all goes well, I will be home in six months. Until
then, I send you this promise: I shall pray for you daily.
Fondly,
William James Smythe
Your Devoted Father

Mother had insisted that no one send word of the house fire to
Father and that if they wrote to him in London, they must not
speak of John's battle with grog and gambling. "He'll hear the
bad news soon enough," she'd said time and again. "He has
enough on his mind, being separated from his family."

If Father had known his family had suffered yet another
blow, would he have refused the king's latest request? Would
he have booked passage on the next ship bound for Boston?
Phillip liked to think that he might have.

He looked up from the letter to study the faces of his family. Mother had tears in her eyes.

"I guess we won't be seeing Father for months, now," Leah
sighed. "I'd so wanted him to be on this ship."

"As had I, Leah. As had I," Mother echoed.

For an instant, Phillip considered flinging his father's neatly
penned letter into the air. Before it fluttered to the floor, he'd
have forced them to acknowledge that caring for three families
—his own, Cousin George's, *and* his brother John's—was too
heavy a burden for a boy his age to bear. He would have
admitted he was tired of holding them all together. *Why must
my future be set aside,* he wanted to cry out, *to secure yours!*

In a heartbeat, he regained control. All was not lost. There was *one* place to find peace, to find solace.

Phillip slid the letter back into its matching envelope and handed it to Mother. He marched stiff-backed from the kitchen.

"Phillip," Leah called.

"Leave him alone, child," he could hear Mother say. "He needs some time by himself."

Phillip lifted the Good Book from the shelf beside the fireplace in the parlor. He would not let them see the frown that furrowed his brow, nor hear his heartfelt plea as he sank heavily onto the rocker near the hearth.

CHAPTER SEVEN

A Death in the Family

"Show me where to find the strength to persist," Phillip whispered.

When the Bible fell open to a random page near the back of the book, Phillip's gaze settled immediately upon 1 Corinthians

10:13: "God is faithful, who will not suffer you to be tempted above that ye are able; but will with the temptation also make a way to escape, that ye may be able to bear it."

He marked the verse with his forefinger, then glanced away to consider its meaning. The big clock near the door *ticked*, and even before it *tocked*, Phillip knew without a doubt that finding this verse had not been an accident. It was a sign. . .an answer straight from God to his recent, fervent prayer.

Gradually, the weariness that clouded his soul and the sadness that hardened his heart vanished. The Lord knew what Phillip could bear and had promised that when trials and tribulations tempted him, He would provide a safe escape.

Phillip knew that he could face the bleak days ahead. He could endure the constant barrage of needs which came at him from all sides. He could stand tall under the pressure of knowing his lifelong dream had been snuffed out like the smothered flame of a candle's wick.

Just as he had promised not to let his father down, Phillip now believed that his Father in heaven would not let him down. Surely nothing that happened in the future could shake this newfound faith.

Sarah and Jake had named their daughter Hope, because she'd come to them at a time when there was so little hope to go around. But Leah and Phillip shared the family's concern over Sarah's health. Their older sister had not fared well during the months since the birth of her first child.

"Hope was a large infant," Phillip's mother explained to

them when Sarah failed to regain her health. "And Sarah's such a tiny little thing."

For as long as they could remember, Phillip and Leah had shared a special bond with Sarah. She'd always been far more than an elder sister. Sarah was their friend. She understood Phillip's yearning to become an apothecary and had spent hours entertaining Leah when the younger girl couldn't leave her bed. Sarah understood better than anyone else in the family Phillip's bitter disappointment when his dreams of the future had been dashed.

Because of their love for their older sister, Leah and Phillip were more than willing to help her care for her little baby. Leah would stop by most mornings and then again in the afternoon. And Phillip managed to take a half hour or so every day on his way home from work at the college to give his weakened sister some time to rest.

"Pour yourself a cup of tea," he advised when he stopped the next evening. "Lie back and rest. I won't take the baby far—I promise." She looked particularly pale, but he made no mention of it.

"I never worry when she's in your care, Phillip," she said softly.

He carried Hope down the porch steps and across Sarah's front yard, humming merrily as he headed for the woods. Hope loved to look up at the canopy of trees, and delighted in the sounds of birds and bugs. Seeing these very ordinary things through her bright, eager eyes gave them a whole new look. Phillip's greatest joy these days came from holding

Sarah's child in his arms. It was as though Hope represented everything innocent and sweet in a world of bitter disappointment.

He took care to choose his moments with her when no one else was around. There was no telling what ridicule he might be forced to endure if anyone saw the way he behaved with his little niece. He made comical faces and ridiculous noises to coax bubbles of laughter from her double-chinned throat.

They walked deep into the forest for nearly a half hour, Phillip pointing out plants and animals, Hope reacting with infantile glee.

"Ah, Hope," he whispered as her long-lashed eyes drank in the sights around her, "there is so much to see, isn't there? So much to learn." He directed her attention to a low-hanging bough. "This is called a fir tree. It stays green the whole year round." He tweaked her chubby cheek. "And you stay *round* the whole year round!"

Pointing to a gnarled trunk, he added, "And this is an oak. When the weather turns cold, it'll lose every one of its shiny green leaves. See the ones way up top, there? It's barely September, and already they've turned gold."

Hope arched her back and reached for the leaf of a wild rose bush. "Bli-voo," she said.

He plucked one of the flowers from the shrub. "We'll give it to your mother. She'll love it."

"Bli-voo," she repeated. "Mlah-flah-smah."

"You don't say!" Phillip grinned in response to the excited babble that passed her lips. Suddenly, he tickled her tummy.

"Hope, I'm trying to be as charitable as I can, but. . .you stink!"

Hope giggled in response to his affectionate playfulness, her pink mouth opened wide with pure joy.

"Come on," he said, starting the long trek back toward the house. "Let's get you home, where your mother can clean up the mess you've made." Phillip couldn't help smiling a self-satisfied smirk, for he knew that with all the rest of the dirty work they demanded of him, this was *one* job the women couldn't ask him to perform!

"I've a surprise for you, Sarah," he called, grinning as he entered the quiet house, "and so does your daughter."

He walked farther into the room, carrying the baby and the single rose. "Come now, Sarah Jane, I've given you a lengthy rest. It's time for you to take your little girl back now." He paused and added, "I'd advise a quick trip to the water trough first thing, though, because Hope needs a good rinsing off."

Still not a sound save the ticking of the clock.

Strange, Phillip thought. *She should be putting supper on the table for Jake by now.* "Sarah?"

The only sound now was the pounding of his heart.

"Sarah. . ."

Silence.

The fear in his voice crackled in the room when he yelled, "Sarah!"

Hope lurched with fright at his sudden, loud shout, and Phillip patted her tiny back reassuringly. "There, there," he whispered, kissing her cheek. "I didn't mean to bellow into your ear. I'm just trying to rouse your lazy mother, that's all, so she'll change your diapers before you get a nasty rash."

There's no reason for concern, he told himself. *You told her to pour herself a cup of tea, and rest.* She'd obviously taken his advice and had fallen asleep. He stepped gingerly into her parlor, so as not to startle her if indeed she was napping.

But Sarah was not in the parlor.

After a quick inspection of each room, Phillip realized she was not in the house at all.

Frantic now, he clutched the baby closer and ran outside, to check the backyard. "This isn't like her," he said, more to himself than to Hope. "She knew I'd taken you into the woods out back. You'd think she would have called to us, told us where she was going."

Just then he spotted Leah running toward them.

When the girl reached the yard, she was gasping for breath. "It's Sarah. Mother found her, unconscious, in a pool of blood. They've taken her to Catherine's. It's closer to the doctor's. Jake's out hunting him down now."

The only word he'd really heard was "blood." Phillipdarted back into the house, his gaze was drawn to the hooked rug on the parlor floor. There, in its center, a large red stain. . .

He looked at Hope, who blinked innocently up at him, oblivious to the gravity of the announcement Leah had just made. "I've got to be with her," he said, handing the baby to his sister.

Phillip ran every step between Sarah's house and Catherine's. He'd been moving so fast for so long that he found it difficult to stop and nearly ran into Dr. Turner.

The big man rarely smiled, so the somber expression on his

ruddy face was no real reason for concern. Still. . .

"Leah says my mother found Sarah," he told the physician. "He said they brought her here."

Dr. Turner nodded. "She's inside, but—"

"She's all right, isn't she? Because I don't think I've ever seen as much blood."

The doctor opened his mouth to answer him, but Mother spoke first. "Phillip, I want you to go back to Sarah's and stay there with Leah and Hope."

"Mother, where's Sarah? She's all right, isn't she?"

Mother stepped onto the porch and put her arms around him.

"She's gone, Phillip," she sobbed into his shoulder. "Just floated away, like a tuft of corn silk on a summer breeze."

Frowning, he held her at arm's length. "Gone? What do you mean, she's gone?"

Dr. Turner pressed a hand to Phillip's back. "Some women are born to have children, and some are not," he said. "Your sister didn't have the strength—"

The boy jerked free of the adults and stomped to the edge of the porch. "Sarah *was* strong!" he insisted. "Why, many's the time I saw her heft sacks of flour and sugar like they weighed nothing. She could manage a team of horses with the best of men. And she—"

"Phillip," Mother interrupted softly, "please don't make a scene. It won't help matters now."

It won't bring her back to life, you mean! he ranted inwardly. Somewhere, deep in his mind, he heard his own hollow voice reciting, *'God is faithful, who will not suffer you*

67

to be tempted above that ye are able; but will with the tempta-
tion also make a way to escape, that ye may be able to bear it.'

Phillip stomped into the house, and his gaze traveled
immediately to where his sister lay, deathly still.

Jake, on one knee beside Sarah, clasped her pale, limp hand
in his strong, tanned one. His dark eyes were swimming with
tears when they met Phillip's, but he said nothing.

"A fine God You are!" Phillip exploded, shaking his fist at
the ceiling. "A fine God, indeed!"

Slowly, Jake stood. "Stop it, Phillip," he growled, his voice
deep and foggy with despair. "If I can bear this, you can, too."

Shamed into stunned silence, Phillip stared into his beloved
brother-in-law's red-rimmed eyes. *If the Lord truly knows our*
limits, Phillip asked himself, *how could He have allowed yet*
another tragedy to strike this family?

Feeling weak-kneed and light-headed, Phillip slumped onto
the nearest stiff-backed chair and held his head in his hands.
What will become of Jake? he wondered. *The man loves Sarah*
more than life itself! And who will mother little Hope now that
Sarah is gone?

Catherine and Hannah huddled near the door, sobbing
softly. He didn't have to look into Mother's face to know how
deeply her daughter's sudden death had affected her. He'd already read the agony etched into her fine features. How would
she endure yet another loss, particularly without the support
of a loving husband?

"The Lord giveth and the Lord taketh away," he heard the
doctor say.

Phillip swallowed the urge to scoff at Turner's attempt to comfort the grieving family. "He does more than enough taking," he muttered under his breath.

He had done everything that had been asked of him, and he'd done it without complaint, despite all it had cost him. He knew without a doubt that he would continue doing the right things, just as he knew he would stand strong now, for his mother, for Jake and Hope and Leah, for Catherine and Thomas and Hannah and Zach. He'd do it because he'd given his father his word, and a Smythe did not go back on his word.

As he stared through teary eyes at Sarah's ashen face, he acknowledged that something of him had died with her, and that something had a name: Faith.

Somewhere, deep in his heart, he held tight to a glimmer of hope that if he did the right things, God would reward him in the end. Through it all, his faith had been strong and sure, because he believed the Lord would repay his hard work by someday letting him live out his dream of becoming an apothecary.

But his father had been forced to sail to London.

The business and the family home were gone.

John seemed lost forever to gambling and grog.

George was dead.

And now Sarah. . .

Phillip stood, straightened his shoulders, and lifted his chin. He glanced around the room, at his mother, at Jake. There was a sturdy roof over their heads and plenty of food to fill their bellies. And each of them had warm coats and boots to see them through the winter.

A sob ached in his throat as tears burned behind his closed eyelids. *I'd give it all up, just to have my Sarah back!*

The foreman at the college had paid him today. Phillip opened his eyes and took a deep breath, slid a penny from his pocket, and handed it to the doctor. "Thank you for your trouble, sir," he said, dismissing the man as he drew his grieving mother into a comforting embrace.

Yes, he would get on with his life. He would help complete Boston's first college, just as he would fetch water and wood for the women in his life. He would do everything he'd promised his father he'd do. . .and then some. . .because he was a man now, and these were things a man would do.

But one thing was sure. Phillip would no longer put childlike faith in a God who made promises He could not keep.

When Phillip returned to Sarah and Jake's home, Leah met him anxiously at the door. "Phillip, what's wrong?" she whispered. "You've been gone so long. I fed Hope and—"

Phillip held up a hand. "I have bad news, Leah. Our Sarah's dead."

"Dead?" Leah's eyes widened. "But. . .but she was fine when they loaded her onto the wagon to bring her to see Dr. Turner. I heard her tell Mother that you were in the woods with Hope."

"The doctor said she wasn't strong enough," Phillip said woodenly. "Oh, Leah!" Phillip sat down on the front step and buried his face in his hands. "What's going to happen to little Hope?"

CHAPTER EIGHT

Danger in the Cave

Every morning on his way to the college, Phillip stopped at the church. The men of the parish had long since repaired the cyclone's damage, and the building now shone brightly in the morning sun.

Behind it, a whitewashed picket fence now surrounded the graveyard.

In the cemetery, a marker for George. And one for Sarah. Three lines of script had been carved into the dull grey granite:

Sarah Donnelley
Beloved wife, mother, daughter, sister
June 1610 - September 1636

Winter had arrived, and its brisk and blustery winds left few things in bloom. But Phillip always managed to find something to place at Sarah's grave. Sometimes, it was a wispy pine branch decorated with a crisp brown cone. Other times, he chose a sprig of shiny holly with bright red berries.

He put a bouquet of boxwood at the foot of the stone that bleak December morning. Down on one knee, he rested a hand upon the marker. "Hope has more teeth now, Sarah," he said softly, "and a body is wise to keep his fingers clear of the sharp little things!" A wistful smile lifted the corners of his mouth. "Jake says all the time how much she looks like you."

And it was true. Hope had inherited the same brown hair and fair complexion. But the similarities went much farther than that. Like her mother, the child could sweeten even the most sour mood with nothing more than a flash of her easy smile. The most striking resemblance could be seen in those long-lashed, emerald-green eyes.

It was a startling likeness that had often stunned Phillip into silence. No matter how carefully he guarded his emotions, the small child seemed able to read his moods. No one but his sister had ever been able to do that. That bit of Sarah's bighearted nature seemed to shine in her daughter's eyes. Phillip sensed that when Hope left baby talk behind, she, like her mother, would know exactly which words would lift a heavy heart.

He wished that Hope could speak now, for he longed to hear words of comfort and reassurance from one who truly understood the dreams that lived in him. "I won't be back for awhile," he said, standing. "It's time to begin working in the cave before and after work. It'll be a tough project to complete, but I expect to have it done in a few weeks."

Dusting dirt and bits of dried grass from the knees of his breeches, he took a step back from the grave. "I miss you, Sarah," he said. Then, annoyed at his own weakness, he angrily swiped away the traitorous tears that had filled his eyes. He walked purposefully toward the path that would lead him to the college.

Finally, the place had been given a name—Harvard, in honor of the Reverend John Harvard. The fancy men of Boston, most of whom had been educated at England's Cambridge University, had decided to build the college so the colony would have an ample supply of educated clergy and lay leadership. Theological and classical studies would form the core of the students' studies, but Harvard's founders believed strongly in the importance of welcoming the new sciences, as well.

It would be a grand institution, indeed, and Phillip wondered if those areas of science would include apothecary—

He forced the thought from his mind. He had been born to a carpenter, and a day laborer was all he'd ever be. To allow himself even a moment of pretending he could become an apothecary was foolhardy. Following in Jake's footsteps had been nothing more than the dream of a silly boy, and he was neither silly nor a dreamer any longer.

Still a spark of hope glowed bright within him. Phillip had a new dream. He would replace his father's business, from the workshop to the smallest tack hammer, before Father returned from England.

Before his father had left for England, Phillip had spent time with his friend White Wolf in a Narragansett village. One of the most fascinating things Phillip had seen there were the huge ovens in which the women baked their bread. Constructed of bricks, the rounded stoves could withstand amazing heat. He used those ovens as a model when he went to build a furnace in the woods near the cave. His furnace would also have to pass the test of many hot fires if it was to help Phillip rebuild his father's dream.

Phillip experimented over several weeks to find just the right combination of materials to make bricks for the firebox. He gathered mud from the creek bed and shaped it by hand, but the cubes never hardened sufficiently. Then he tried mixing sand with the clay. He used too much the first time and not enough the next. In order for the mixture to harden properly, he discovered that it had to start out the thick, mucky consistency of stew broth and be allowed to dry slowly in the sun.

For that, Phillip needed the forms that Thomas had caught him making. He'd found plenty of lumber in the aftermath of the storm, but the one thing in short supply were nails to hold the molds together. It was a tiresome, time-consuming process, waiting for the clay to dry enough to allow him to remove the nails and build more shapers.

By his calculations, Phillip would need no fewer than five hundred bricks to build an oven large enough to accommodate the flat-bottomed bowls he'd made in much the same way he'd created the bricks. But after weeks of work, he was down to making his last batch of bricks.

As he waited for the bricks to dry, he tested various methods of bonding them together. One day he complained to Jake about his half-dozen unsuccessful mixtures. His brother-in-law suggested Phillip try daub, a compound made in Ireland out of sand, water, limestone. . .and a bit of manure.

Each night, before weariness forced him to head home to his narrow cot, Phillip draped a greased tarp over his work. It slowed the drying process by cutting the air circulation a mite, but it protected the oven from rain or dew until it had a chance to dry thoroughly.

He'd chosen the site for his oven with careful deliberation, knowing that its proximity to the cave would simplify his work once the oven was finished. For now, it saved time as he trekked back and forth between the oven and the cave. Using the chisel he'd once borrowed for protection in that cave, Phillip loosened the ore buried in the cave's cold stone walls.

Finally the day arrived when he would lay the final row of bricks. In three or four days, when this last layer dried, he would build a roaring fire in its belly and test its durability. If the experiment was successful, he would be able to move on to the next phase of his plan: smelting the iron he'd mined from the cave.

All through his workday and all the way home, he plotted

the placement of each brick, the spreading of the mortar. He could barely wait to finish his household chores and his supper so that he could head for the woods!

"Phillip," his mother said as she passed him a second helping of stew, "you're gulping down your meal like a starving wolf cub." Sighing, she added, "I do wish Sam Paulsen wouldn't work you so hard."

"I'm fine, Mother," he mumbled around a mouthful of corn bread. "Hard work builds strong backs and strong character." Through narrowed eyes, he leveled an angry stare at his brother John. "Something a few more of us could stand to develop."

Glaring, John aimed his forefinger at Phillip. "Don't start with me, stinkpot, or I'll take you out back and tan your hide."

"I'd like to see you try," the younger brother challenged.

"So, you want another taste of the medicine I gave you in the woods?"

"You might find I won't be such a willing patient this time. You might even find you've met your match, you coward!"

John stood so abruptly that he toppled his stool, fists and jaw clenched and eyes glowing with murderous rage.

"Boys!" Mother said firmly.

Thomas gasped, his blue eyes wide with fright. "They're going to start up where they left off in the woods that day."

"What day?" Mother wanted to know.

Phillip zeroed in on his cousin. "Hush," he warned in a whisper, "or it'll be *your* hide that's tanned."

Mother persisted. "All right, boys, I'll leave you to your

little secrets. But I will not tolerate such behavior at Catherine's table. Is that clear?"

She jabbed a forefinger in John's direction. "You will take your seat, young man, and keep a civil tongue in your head." Aiming the digit at Phillip, she added, "And you will control your temper. There was nothing loving about the words you just spoke to your brother."

John and Phillip stared down at their plates and the meal ended in strained silence. But Phillip appreciated the sympathetic squeeze Leah gave his arm as she passed by him on her way to the kitchen. The situation with John was too much. He couldn't wait to get back to the solitude of the cave.

Phillip had been making such a racket hammering the chisel into the stone, that he hadn't heard anyone enter the cave. It wasn't until he saw the huge, hovering shadow that darkened the cold wall beside him that he realized he was not alone.

He turned quickly and faced John. "What's wrong with you," Phillip demanded, "skulking around like a thief in the night?"

"Didn't mean to scare you."

It was hard to read John's expression in the shadows thrown by the lantern, but judging by the tone of his voice, his brother was still angry.

"What do you want?"

"The better question is, what do *you* want in this wretched cave?"

Phillip resumed his chiseling. "It's none of your business."

"I'm making it my business," his brother said, grabbing

Phillip by the scruff of the neck and jerking him so hard that the tools dropped to the floor. "Tell me what you're digging for, or the beating I gave you last time will seem like a love tap compared to this one!"

John raised his fist.

"Go ahead," Phillip said calmly. "Throw your best punch, John." He glanced around the cave. "I don't see anyone who'd try and stop you."

It seemed all the inspiration John needed. He pounded Phillip as if he were in a fight to the death.

"You really hate me, don't you?" Phillip asked.

"And why wouldn't I? You delight in making me look like a fool in front of my wife and mother."

The thought seemed to incite John, and he came at Phillip with new fury and vigor. Still, Phillip refused to return even one of John's hard blows.

"Don't just stand there," his brother bellowed. "Defend yourself, why don't you?"

"I don't need my fists to swat away a pesky mosquito," Phillip countered.

"Fight back, I tell you, or I'll send you to join our sister!"

Phillip's eyes burned with disgust and revulsion. John's callous mention of Sarah's death lit the fuse of the bomb of rage smoldering in Phillip's heaving chest. John's face blanched at the rage in his brother's eyes. Numbed with fear, he staggered backward, tripped on a pile of iron nuggets, and went sprawling.

"Send me to be with her, you say? I'd welcome it," Phillip

thundered, "for God took His best to be with Him."

John stared up into his younger brother's bloodied face. "Took His best to be with Him?" he repeated. "And left me behind. Are you insinuating I'm so far gone even the Lord wouldn't want me?"

No. That's not what I'm insinuating, Phillip thought. But he was too tired to respond.

His brother staggered from the cave and didn't look back. "Took His best to be with Him," John mumbled as he went.

Slowly, Phillip flexed his aching muscles, and ran his tongue around the inside of his bruised lips. Shaking his head, he lifted the chisel and set it firmly against the hard cave wall.

CHAPTER NINE

A Change for the Good

John sat on the gravelly bank of the Mystic River and held his head in his hands. Through his fingers, he could see moonbeams dancing on the water's inky surface. Now and again a hungry fish nibbled at the shallow beach that followed the waterway, sending a new pattern of light skimming across the river's skin.

This was the place Phillip had introduced him to soon after his move to Boston. "I come here when I'm worried or sad or afraid," his brother had said. "It's a good place to think."As in so many things, Phillip had been right.

What has become of you? John demanded, pressing his knuckles into his forehead. *How did things get so out of control!*

The answer was right in his shirt pocket, in the form of an IOU.

He'd been hurt by the cyclone's damaging winds and flood waters more than he'd cared to admit. John had built a sturdy house in Boston. He'd gone to work with George and his father. He'd had everything a man could ask from life.

And then in the space of an hour, it was gone. All gone. The house, the business, even Cousin George. As a result, his father had been forced to board a London-bound boat in the hopes of earning enough money to begin again.

"You can make fast money down at the harbor," a co-worker had told John. *It all started because I desired to get my hands on a lot of money in a hurry,* John admitted to himself.

"Nothing worthwhile comes to a man easily," his father had said time and again. He'd also said, "If a job's worth doing, it's worth doing right." And "You reap what you sow."

Well, you've planted an entire field of weeds, John told himself, *worthless, good-for-nothing weeds.*

That first night when he'd accompanied Frederick down to

the shoddy building where the bets were made, John had been disgusted by the sights and smells and sounds. The men who gambled near Boston's bay cursed and bellowed, sang bawdy songs, and roughhoused mercilessly.

Something had told him to leave. Immediately. Something had told him nothing good could come of time spent in that brightly lit, gaudy place.

But before he could find a polite was to bid them farewell, Frederick had shoved a huge mug of grog into his hand, clapped a huge hand on his back, and introduced him to the gamblers. "This is my good friend, John Smythe," the big man had said. "He'll be joinin' us from now on." The man's look told John, "If you leave us now, we'll see it as a slap in the face."

John remembered how embarrassed he'd felt when Frederick had asked, "How much will you wager this night, John m'boy?" He knew gambling was wrong, but he didn't want to disappoint his friends. And he was desperate for a way to rebuild a home for his family.

He'd shrugged, uncertain how the games were played. Grinning sheepishly, he'd said, "I don't rightly know. . . ."

Frederick's hand had landed on his back again with a dull thud. "Ain't he the spit-polished young'un, though?" he asked the men, laughing long and loud.

The jibes seemed good-natured enough to inspire John to join in on the laughter. Inspired him to swallow a mouthful of the bitter grog, too.

Soon, he'd downed several mugs of the mixture. His head reeled and his stomach roiled. Good sense dimmed with every drink. All his life, he'd done the right thing. He'd said a prayer of thanks to God for the morning. Had done his best at whatever job was expected of him. Had shared whatever he could afford to with those less fortunate. He had chosen a quiet and lovely girl to be his bride and had worked hard to give her— and the beautiful son she bore him—all that they deserved.

He would have given her a handful of coins that night—if he hadn't stopped at the harbor on his way home. Next morning, when he woke in the musty warehouse, his head aching and his gut groaning, the money was gone. He'd lost it. . .every penny.

"Not to worry!" Frederick had assured him. "That's the way the games go. One night, you're a loser. The next night, you've a pocket full of silver!"

John had gone straight to work, and on his way to the harbor that night, he'd stopped at his house. There he'd told his wife the first of many lies. "The foreman asked me to work over," he said, unable to meet her eyes. "There was no way to get a message to you. I'm sorry if you worried."

She'd wrapped him in a comforting hug. "I was worried, at first," Hannah had admitted. "But after some thinking, I realized what must have happened. And you must be exhausted, after two long days of hard labor! Let me heat the kettle. You can take a warm soak in the tub while I serve you up a big bowl of mutton stew."

Guilt had hammered in his heart. He'd held her at arm's length, just in case the after-effects of the previous night still clung to his breath or his clothing. "Can't stay," he'd said, continuing his lie. "They want me back at the college as soon as I fill my belly."

"But John," Hannah had whispered. "Zach and I miss you so."

It was *for* Hannah and Zach that he must return to the harbor, John had told himself. He must win back the money he'd lost!

That night, he'd won a few of the games. It had only taken an hour to win back all he'd lost the night before. But ale and the taunting of his new friends tempted him to continue. He'd awakened the next morning in far worse shape than the day before.

I'll beat those games if it kills me! he'd decided.

Night after night, he'd played. . .and lost. And day after day, he'd walked around in a drunken blur.

"What's going on?" Phillip had demanded one day as they worked side by side on the main building of the college. "I heard Hannah complaining to Mother about how much time you're away from home. She thinks you're here, working, and Mother does, too. Why, the two of them are about to start up a petition to close down the operation because the foreman is driving you like a slave!"

John had said nothing, hoping that Phillip would stop asking questions. Instead his younger brother had continued.

"You stink to high heaven, and you look like death warmed over. I know full well you haven't been here every night. Why, you haven't been here *any* night! What's going on?" he repeated.

John had admitted everything to Phillip.

"Then quit," his brother had said.

"It's not that easy. I've borrowed from every man at the harbor, it seems. I can't quit. Not 'til I win back enough to repay them."

"I have some money saved up," the boy had offered. "I can help you pay them back."

John shook his head as he remembered how he hadn't even hesitated to take his younger brother's hard-earned money. "How much, Phillip? How much do you have?"he'd asked eagerly.

But the foreman had interrupted before his brother could name an amount. "You're not being paid to gossip like a couple of old biddies," he'd bellowed. "Get back on your feet and pick up your tools. There are twenty men waiting in line who'd take your jobs on short notice, and give thanks to the Almighty for it, I'll have you know!"

The brothers had gone back to work. After an hour or so, John had said under his breath, "I can't take your money, Phillip. But thank you for offering."

Phillip had shrugged. "I'd do anything for you, John. You know that."

As the days turned into weeks and the weeks became months, John had watched the changes in Phillip. Once, the boy's eyes had beamed with quiet admiration when he looked into his big brother's face. Now, smoldering disgust simmered there.

John sighed as he thought about how many things he wished

he had done differently. If only he had been willing to wait. If only he'd never gone to the wharf in the first place. If only he'd never lied to Hannah.

He felt rather than saw the morning's slow birth. The sun's rays warmed his face and hands, brightened the treetops, opened up the sky.

An eagle screamed overhead as a fat rabbit hopped down the smooth slope, her bunnies close on her heels. Cottony clouds sailed silently by.

No matter which way John looked, he felt, rather than saw, the life that was this land. "Thank you for this glorious place," he prayed. "Thank you for this beautiful morning."

He opened his eyes, unable to continue. He didn't deserve God's ear. Not now. Not after all he'd done—after all the grief he'd caused those who loved him during the past year.

And Phillip—Phillip amazed him. Every day but Sunday, he worked from dawn to dusk at the college, doing his own work and covering for John's mistakes, too. Then in the dark of night, he ground out another grueling shift in the bowels of that cave.

Suddenly John remembered what he'd done to Phillip in that cave. Horror-struck that he could do such a thing, John hung his head in shame.

" 'My confusion is continually before me, and the shame of my face hath covered me,' " he quoted from the Psalms. His pain and torment were deserved, John believed, recalling a verse from Ezekiel: "Thus saith the Lord God; Behold, I have spoken in my jealousy and in my fury, because ye have borne the shame of the heathen."

John fell to his knees in a pool of sunlight, humbled by the awesome power of God's love. Even after all he'd done to hurt those who loved him, he felt the Lord's forgiveness, as warm and comforting as the beams of the sun. Remembering those verses, he realized, had not been an accident. The Almighty had brought them to mind to warn him that continuing on this path was dangerous—and to remind him that it was never too late to begin again.

" 'Be of good courage,' " John prayed from a Psalm, " 'and he shall strengthen your heart, all ye that hope in the Lord.' "

John knew what he had to do, and knew that he had to do it *now*.

CHAPTER TEN
The Last Goodbye

Phillip stood back and surveyed his oven. None of his bricks were flat-sided and square-cornered, like those he was using at the college. And because he'd done all the work in the black of night, he hadn't seen that the mortar oozed from between them and had dried that way in a few places. *It's crude, at best,*

he admitted, frowning to himself, *but God willing, it'll get the job done.*

He ran his hand along the oven's outer wall, nodding. "Yes, it'll do the job," he said aloud.

"What is the purpose of this giant pile of stone?"

Phillip lurched with fright at the sudden interruption. He whirled around, fists clenched in the fight-ready position to defend himself. Just as suddenly, he relaxed, for the voice belonged to his old friend, White Wolf.

"It is. . .interesting," the Indian said, smiling. "Tell me, what will you cook in this oven?"

Phillip took a few steps closer to the Narragansett. Pointing toward the cave, he said, "I'll melt down the ore I mined in there, and when it hardens, I'll take it to Salem, where Mr. Martin will make new tools for my father."

White Wolf sat on the cold, hard ground and clasped his hands together. "And how is your friend Geoffrey?"

Phillip sat across from him. "I got a letter several months ago. He's lonely right now, but things will turn around." Grinning, he added, "They always do, where Geoffrey's concerned."

The Indian nodded, smiling serenely. "It has been many moons since last we talked, my young friend. Tell me, how is your family?"

Phillip took a deep breath. So much had happened in the year since he'd seen White Wolf that he didn't know where to begin.

He started with the cyclone and told the Indian about everything that had happened in its aftermath. By the time he finished telling it, Phillip's lips and eyes had narrowed with resentment and regret.

"Your anger is understandable," White Wolf said, "but your bitterness will only bring you trouble."

Phillip quirked an eyebrow in surprise. "There's nothing left to life but hard work," he said. "I think a little bitterness is expected."

But the Indian shook his head. "Your sister, Leah. Is she still ill?"

"Well, no. Actually, she's better than she's ever been in her life."

"And your mother. Is she in good health?"

"Yessss."

"Your father's leg—the one that was so seriously injured when he fell from the grain shed roof—has it healed?"

"It has. But he's in London, remember, trying to earn enough money to rebuild the business. I can't imagine how distressed he'll be when he returns to find he'll also have to build us a new house, thanks to John."

"Ah," White Wolf said. "*This* is the cause of your bitterness. You are angry with your brother." The Indian leaned elbows on knees and furrowed his brow. "What has he done that is so unforgivable, my friend?"

Phillip spat out John's recent history with venomous speed. The gambling, the grog, the greed that had caused both, and the lies his brother had told came pouring out. "It was *his* fault the house burned down!" Phillip shouted. "If he hadn't taken up with those. . .those *misfits*. . ."

Grimacing, he clenched his fists. "They burned the house down to warn him they meant to get their money back, no matter what. Did it make any difference? No! He kept right on drinking and gambling, kept right on borrowing until he owes so much he'll likely never repay them." He pounded the earth with a fist.

"What can these men do?"

"They can appeal to the elders and pledge young Zach to indentured servitude."

"But he's no more than a papoose!"

Phillip's eyes narrowed. "Who could be so low that he would risk his child's future by his reckless ways?"

The Indian looked skyward. A deep line was etched on his forehead when he said, "I see a time when many may do just that in this land." He met Phillip's eyes again. "But that which may happen hundreds of years from this time is no help to you now."

Phillip took a great gulp of air, held it a moment, and summoned his calm. "There's no telling what they'll do next. Why, they might just roast the lot of us to show him how serious they are about collecting on their debt!"

White Wolf sat in silence for a long time. "These marks of battle on your face and hands. . .your brother did this to you?"

Phillip stared numbly as he opened and closed, opened and closed his fists. "He did," he said at last.

"And you did nothing to defend yourself."

He looked up quickly, surprised. "How did you know?"

White Wolf's smile was tinged with sadness. "You are a brave young man who is fully able to make marks of battle on any man who would attack you. But when that man is your brother. . ."

He shouldn't have been surprised, for White Wolf had been blessed with an understanding heart. Phillip only sighed in response.

The Indian stood and headed for the cave. "Come," he said. "Show me the work you have done." Standing in the yawning entrance, he stopped and grinned, "And then I will tell you about my son."

It was the first time since beginning the mining operation that Phillip got absolutely no work done. He and White Wolf talked for hours, and when the black, starry sky brightened to a deep purple, the Indian rose. "I must go now, before someone from your village sees me."

The incident that had occurred a year earlier still loomed large in Phillip's mind. He'd never come that close to witnessing a cold-blooded murder. If the Lord hadn't intervened that night. . .

Phillip swallowed hard. Anger coursed through him as he remembered Cousin George, Sarah, the devastation of the storm, and John's change of character. *God had nothing to do with saving White Wolf from the mob,* he decided. Rather, it had been Phillip's father who had forestalled the catastrophe. *The Lord may have created the heavens and the earth,* Phillip fumed, *but He's done little else since to help His children!*

"What puts the fury back into your eyes, Phillip?" White Wolf asked.

For a moment, they walked in silence on the woodland path that would lead the Indian home. Finally, Phillip said, "I have lost my faith, White Wolf. I no longer believe there is a God in the heavens."

The Narragansett stopped in his tracks. "And why is that?"

Lifting his chin in defiance, the boy answered, "Because the world is simply too vile and ugly a place. It's absolute proof, if you ask me, that there can be no such thing as a God of mercy and love!"

White Wolf nodded somberly. "There is truth in what you say, my young friend." He crossed both arms over his broad chest and stood facing the rising sun. "Sometimes, the world in which we live makes us blind to the work of the Great Spirit."

Phillip frowned and stared balefully ahead.

The Indian ignored the boy's anger and continued in a patient, calm voice. "But the Creator is *not* heartless, Phillip. The earth often seems a cold, bleak place because of the humans who live upon it."

"What! You're saying it's *our* fault that things are in such chaos!"

"That's what I'm saying, yes." White Wolf took a step forward and stroked the bark of a birch tree. "You see, Phillip, the Creator made the earth and all that surrounds it—the trees and the soil from which they grow. Those trees protect us from the sun's heat and provide us with wood for our homes and fuel to burn in our stoves so we can cook our food and warm our bodies."

He nodded toward the Mystic River. "He made the fish in the water." Pointing at the sky, he added, "Every bird that wings toward heaven, and the animals that give their flesh to fill our bellies and to be sewn into shirts and shoes and canoes."

White Wolf lay a hand upon Phillip's shoulder. "But of all these things He gave, His greatest gift was His only Son. Could a God whose heart was hard give such a gift? We are all God's children, and we must have patience and forbearance to welcome home the prodigal."

"You mean John?"

The Indian sighed. "You are young to bear such weight alone, my friend, but the reason you can bear it is because you were *made* to bear it."

"My point, exactly!" Phillip interrupted. "If there *was* a God, and if He *was* kind and forgiving, would He make me strong and my brother weak? Would he brew up storms that would destroy all that He made—that would destroy all that the humans He created made?"

The Indian kept his gaze locked on Phillip's. His dark eyes were hard and his mouth stern when he said, "Do not let these events harden your heart, my friend. Your heart is the only thing that separates you from the beasts of the field."

Phillip frowned with confusion. Shrugging, he said, "I don't know what He wants from me. Surely all that has happened hasn't been a test of my manhood. And if it has been a test, surely I've passed by now!"

White Wolf only shook his head. "The English missionary who taught me to read also taught me this about our God: 'Put on the whole armour of God, that ye may be able to stand against the wiles of the devil, for we wrestle not against flesh and blood, but against principalities, against powers, against the rulers of the darkness of this world.' "

Phillip's frown deepened. "I don't under—"

"The armour of God," White Wolf repeated. " 'Having your loins girt with truth, and having on the breastplate of righteousness; and your feet shod with the preparation of the gospel of peace. . . . The helmet of salvation, and the sword of the Spirit, which is the word of God. . . .

" 'Above all, taking the shield of faith, wherewith ye shall be able to quench all the fiery darts of the wicked.' "

White Wolf extended his hand to Phillip, who took it as the Indian had taught him. He clasped the Narragansett's right forearm with his right hand as the man did the same to Phillip. "I will go now, and leave you to think on these things. Your Creator has not forsaken you, Phillip. If He seems lost to you, it is only because you have forgotten where to find Him."

I have forgotten, Phillip thought. *In fact, I wonder if I ever really knew where to find Him.*

"He is there," White Wolf said, his forefinger gently jabbing Phillip's chest, "in your heart, and there," he added, touching the boy's temple, "in your mind. He's been there all along, but the evil elements of the world have hidden Him from you." Having said this, he turned to leave.

Phillip didn't want his friend to leave. He had no one else

to talk with, to seek guidance from. No one else would offer advice and point out the right path. He hadn't consciously felt alone before now, but as the Indian began walking down the woodland path toward the Narragansett village, a sorrowful sense of isolation surrounded the boy.

His body had grown considerably since he'd met the Indian. He'd been doing a man's work with a man's mind-set for more than a year, and it had broadened and strengthened him in body and in mind. He stood taller than most boys his age— taller, even, than some of Boston's full-grown men. So Phillip didn't understand the tears that burned behind his eyelids, the sob that ached in his throat.

He resisted the urge to cry, squared his shoulders, and called out, "When will I see you next, White Wolf?"

The Indian did not cease his steady pace, nor did he turn to face Phillip. "When we are both dead, we will meet again in the Great Sky."

No, Phillip cried mentally, *I can't wait a lifetime to speak with you again.*

"Think of all I have said, Phillip," White Wolf said. "I am not a wise man, like my father before me, but I know this much. You are loved by the Creator."

Later, as he performed his duties at the college, Phillip would consider the Indian's advice. And more than likely, he'd consider them again as he did his chores at home. Even now, before having a chance to weigh the wisdom of White Wolf's words, Phillip knew he'd find solace in them, for he'd never known the Indian to speak anything but the truth. It had been a pleasure. . .no. . .a *blessing* to have known this great man.

Phillip lifted his arm in a silent farewell. "I will miss you, White Wolf," he whispered. "I am honored to have had you call me friend."

He couldn't possibly have seen Phillip's last wave, for White Wolf had never turned around. Couldn't have heard his soft words of endearment, for he was nearly out of sight now in the dim, dense forest.

Yet White Wolf's hand went up and his voice floated back to Phillip on the early morning breeze. "You need not miss me, for I am there, always, in your thoughts." He turned, stopped, lowered his hand. "I am honored to call *you* friend."

For several moments, Phillip stared at the place where he'd last seen White Wolf. It was true that the Indian's words, his voice, his actions would always live in Phillip's heart.

But he would miss him, anyway.

Chapter Eleven

Father's Dream

Phillip had learned a lot in his visit to the Narragansett village all those months ago. While Black Eagle and Jake had discussed herbs and roots and remedies, he had stood back and watched the women scrape the fat and tissue from still-warm animal hides.

"It will become too stiff to work with," White Wolf had explained, "if they wait until the carcasses cool. There are few whose hands are skilled enough to perform this task," the Indian continued. "These are well-respected women, for this work is one of the most prized of female virtues."

Nodding, Phillip had focused on pelts that had already been cleaned of meat and were tied by all four corners to saplings and stretched taut to dry in the summer's sunny breezes. Careful and consistent hammering of the dried skins would ensure supple hides, which could be sewn into garments or made into shoes. It might take up to two weeks for the material to be ready to be worked on.

"Why such effort?" he'd asked an Indian woman.

"My labors are a gift to my husband," she'd said, without looking up from her work. "Game is scarce and the hunts are long. This will ensure soft skin against his, even if I am not with him."

Remembering that conversation, Phillip smiled. He had no intention of creating anything quite so fancy with his pelts. His only purpose was to produce enough leather to create the bellows that would control the airflow through his furnace.

Now he was glad he'd paid attention while watching Geoffrey's father perform the chores of a blacksmith. While he wouldn't begin to think of himself as skilled enough to even be an apprentice smith, he did know how to build a stove that would melt the iron he'd dug from the cave's walls.

Phillip inspected the smelting pot he'd created of the same material he'd mixed to make bricks for the oven. On top of the pot, he carved a hole through which he'd pour red-hot ore. He'd made a clay plug, too, which would be popped out once the iron was heated to a liquid state.

Clay-lined wood troughs would allow him to pour the melted metal into molds carved of wood and also lined with clay. His skimmer would remove the slag that would float to the top of the molten metal. And the rest of the wood he'd scavenged from all over town following the cyclone would fuel the fire that made everything possible.

Finally, everything was ready. During the long walk from the college to Cousin Catherine's house, Phillip thought about the work that lay ahead. As he performed his usual household chores, he plotted the order in which he'd do things. The project would flow as smoothly as the hot iron—provided there were no surprises along the way.

As he ate his supper of roasted fowl and boiled potatoes, Phillip considered those surprises. The whole idea was, at best, a dangerous undertaking. The smelting pot could tip, spilling liquid ore onto him. The stove could collapse under the strain of high-fired heat. Any number of hazards awaited him at the mouth of the cave.

He hoped the precautions he'd taken to prevent them would protect him *and* the woods from harm. But despite the risk, he would turn this dream into a reality.

As soon as his evening chores were finished, Phillip ran to the cave and began organizing his work. Suddenly, he knew someone had joined him. He didn't need to turn around to know who it was. "What do you want, John?" he demanded calmly.

"It sends chills up my spine, the way you do that."

He faced his older brother. "The way I do what?"

John shrugged. "You never even turned around. And I hadn't said a word. How did you know it was me?"

As he bent to retrieve the nuggets of ore he'd mined, Phillip gave the question a moment's thought. Squatting, he shrugged one shoulder and said, "Some men cast recognizable shadows, that's all." He dumped the iron into the wheelbarrow he'd made of wood scraps and eyed his brother warily.

"What do you want?" he asked again, frowning. "Surely you're not in the mood for another fight."

Even in the dim light of the lanterns, Phillip saw John wince.

"Mother gave me quite a tongue-lashing for doing that to you, I'll have you know."

"How'd she know you did it? *I* never told her."

John shook his head and pocketed both hands. "She knew. Somehow, she just knew." He stood quietly for a moment. "You're a lot like her that way—keen observers, the both of you."

He didn't need a clock to know the hours were quickly ticking away. Phillip's frown intensified. "I have a lot to do, John, and very little time to get it done. Now, either tell me what you want, or step out of the way so I can get busy."

His brother closed his eyes. "I. . .I've come to apologize."

Phillip straightened from his work, his eyes wide with shock. "Apologize! To me?" A short, angry laugh exited his lips. "Whatever for?"

John took a deep breath and, after a lengthy pause, plunged in. "For the beatings. For the drinking and the gambling that caused those harbor hobos to burn down the house." He fell to his knees and held his head in his hands. "For making you work double hard at the college to keep my wages coming in. For being a weak, spineless. . ."

John continued to speak, but Phillip's attention was caught by something he hadn't seen in months. *What's that?* Phillip asked himself as something shimmered in the lamplight on the back of his brother's hand. *Are those tears I see?*

Suddenly he realized that John was overcome with heart-felt, rib-racking sobs. "I went up to the overlook," John said between gasps. "You'll think I've gone mad, Phillip, but I declare it's true. God spoke to me there. And I've seen the error of my ways."

After a long, cleansing breath, he continued. "There's no way I can undo all the damage I've caused. But I can try to make things right. . .given time."

Phillip regarded him through narrowed eyes. "It took time to do this damage, John. It can't be undone with a few tears and one measly apology."

Slowly, John got to his feet. "You're right, Phillip, and I don't blame you for not trusting me. But I can prove, at least, that my intentions are pure." He shook his head and struggled for a moment to still his trembling lips. "I made things right with Hannah. I told her everything—confessed it all."

He met Phillip's eyes. "She gave me the ruby ring and ear-bobs that her grandmother gave her and told me to buy back my dignity with them. And so I handed the family heirlooms over to those louts in repayment of my debt." He exhaled loudly. "I'm free of them, Phillip. Finally, I'm rid of their threats."

Phillip's frown intensified. He crossed both arms over his chest and planted his feet shoulder-width apart. "It's a good beginning your wife has bought for you," he said, the cold edge of his words echoing in the cool interior of the cave.

Phillip stood staring in silence for several moments. His brother had come begging forgiveness. *Do you have it in you to give it?* Phillip asked himself. *After all the damage he's done, can you trust him to change?*

John said nothing. He looked haunted and haggard, as if the burden of his destructive behavior had suddenly become too heavy to bear. His eyes, which once glowed bright with good cheer, were dim now with sorrow, and the corners of the mouth that had so often curved with good-natured smiles now turned down in a scowl that would look more at home on the face of a creaking old man.

Where is the John who taught me to set a snare? Phillip wondered. *Where is the brother who showed me how to bait a fishing hook?* Certainly, he was not the man who had guzzled grog and gambled away his wife's inheritance. Just as surely, he was not this stricken man who stood before him now.

"Ye ought rather to forgive him, and comfort him, lest perhaps such a one should be swallowed up with overmuch sorrow, wherefore I beseech you that ye would confirm your love toward him. For to this end. . .I might know the proof of you."

Phillip's ears felt hot, his palms damp as he tried in vain to moisten his parched lips with a suddenly dry tongue. His heart swelled with emotion, and it took all the strength he could muster to keep the threatening tears at bay.

There was a good chance that what Phillip had just witnessed was nothing more than a scene from a well-plotted play. Perhaps John had learned, when he'd taken lessons in drinking and gambling, to put on the face of a sorrowful man—a face that would inspire pity. Or perhaps he'd discovered how to ply undeserved forgiveness from loved ones he'd harmed.

But then there was an equal chance that John's tears had been sincere.

On that chance, Phillip crossed the small space that separated him from John and held the chisel out to his brother. "There's a lot to do here, and I daresay we could get twice the work done in half the time. . .if you'd lend me a hand."

John glanced from his brother's eyes to the tool and back again. A shaky smile brightened his face as he took it. "Is this the same one you borrowed to fend off painted Indian warriors?"

Phillip grinned and nodded. "It is."

His brother tightened his grip on the smooth wooden handle. "It has quite a history, then, I'd say. Maybe it's a good thing inanimate objects can't talk."

Now there's the John I used to know! Phillip thought. "On the contrary," he said, "if it could talk, you'd be entertained long into the night. Now what say you dig some more ore out of that wall while I load it into the wheelbarrow?"

John walked purposefully toward the place where Phillip had been standing when he entered the cave. "You never did tell me what's going on here," he said, striking mallet to chisel to loosen iron from the stone.

"We're going to make Father's dreams come true," Phillip said matter-of-factly.

The hand that held the mallet froze above the wood handle. "Dreams?" John said. "I didn't realize Father *had* any dreams."

Phillip only smiled knowingly. "Neither did he," he said, wheeling the cart out of the cave. "Neither did he."

CHAPTER TWELVE

Adventures in Salem

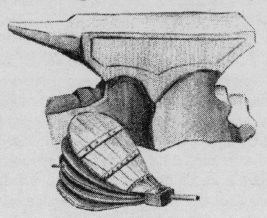

The brothers found that, even working as a two-man team, it took a whole night to make just one ingot. The brick-sized chunks of pig iron, once cooled, were removed from the molds.

Leah suspected something was up. "I haven't seen you and John acting this close since before Father left," she said to

Phillip one evening before supper. "What are you up to? Won't you *please* tell me? I promise I won't tell anyone."

Phillip hesitated, not sure how to respond.

Leah looked up at him with eyes full of mischief. "If you don't tell me, I can always follow you out to the cave and find out for myself," she threatened. "For that matter, I could tell Mother, and then whatever surprise it is the two of you are working on would be ruined."

Phillip sighed. He knew Leah was perfectly capable of doing exactly what she said. He also knew she was very good at keeping secrets. "All right," he said. "I'll tell, but you have to promise not to let anyone know—not by so much as a look."

As soon as she found out, Leah insisted on helping out. While her brothers wouldn't let her dig for ore or help pour the metal when it was melted, they weren't about to turn down molasses cookies. "I'll make them while I'm taking care of Hope over at Jake's house," Leah said. "You'll need *something* to keep up your strength." She also did Phillip's evening chores so that he and John could get to work earlier.

After three weeks, Phillip and John finally managed to create the needed number of ingots. They got together with Leah the next evening so they could tell Mother what they had been up to.

"I am so proud of you boys," she said. "Your father will be thrilled. And Leah. It is such a blessing to worry about what mischief you might be getting into rather than worrying about whether you will have the strength to get out of bed. Your good health is such an answer to prayer." She gathered all three of her children in a huge hug.

"Now," she said. "One of you boys needs to drive those ingots to Salem."

"Phillip should make the trip," John insisted. "He's been carrying the load alone for so long, a day's ride to Salem will be a well-deserved holiday. And if he has to stay longer, I can cover for him at work. We all know he's done that often enough for me in the past year," he added ruefully.

The next morning, Phillip took off with his brother's rickety cart attached to the old mare. As he traveled through the outskirts of Boston, he wondered if his friend Geoffrey had changed as much as he had during the past year.

Last time he'd seen him, Geoffrey had stood no more than five feet tall and weighed no less than one hundred fifty pounds. His unruly flaming orange hair curled out in all directions, and the freckles that dotted his nose and cheeks made him seem eternally in need of a good face-scrubbing. What would their months apart have done to Geoffrey's appearance?

Perhaps he won't even recognize me, Phillip mused. *I'm nearly eight inches taller than when he left for Salem, and almost fifty pounds heavier.* Since there was no one on the road to see it, Phillip flexed his biceps and said to himself, "Hard work and long hours, that's what made a man of you!"

Leah had packed him a basket full of airy batter biscuits and heavy corn bread, thick slices of mutton, and the legs of two roasted chickens. She'd filled a jar with water, too, along with a slab of cherry cobbler sweetened with molasses sugar.

It should have been enough to last him to Salem and back

again. Phillip didn't know quite how it happened, but he'd eaten every bite even before he was halfway to Salem! *Your stomach will be complaining long and loud by the time you get to Geoffrey's,* he told himself. *Perhaps Mrs. Martin has a pot of her famous venison stew bubbling in the fireplace.*

To distract himself from tantalizing thoughts of food, he passed the last hours of his trip singing "Wake, Awake," a hymn he'd learned as a small boy. He hummed "Lo, How a Rose E'er Blooming" for awhile, then sang "All Hail, Adored Holy Trinity" at the top of his lungs, stopping only because a crow circled over the wagon, caw-cawing her opinion of his caterwauling.

At last, the sights Geoffrey had described in his letter came into view. Huts, not unlike those in the Narragansett village, stood among more modern houses built of wood and tile. Now and again, Phillip spotted homes like the one his family had lived in before the fire. They stood one-story high and were topped off with a thatched roof. Each had a door in the center that was flanked by a many-paned window.

He guided the cart down the rutted street, avoiding men on horseback and ladies on foot. For a town with less than half Boston's population, Salem seemed an amazing, busy place.

Suddenly, a mangy dog stepped in front of the cart. "Whoa," Phillip said to the horse. "Whoa, there." The mutt seemed oblivious to the comings and goings of the humans around him, and when he reached the other side of the road, he flopped in a graceless heap on the porch of the grain shed.

A hatless, bearded gent had stopped his grey speckled mare

to avoid mangling the same muddy canine. "There ought to be a law," he muttered, frowning at the pup. "Someone could get hurt, trying to avoid things like that."

Phillip nodded his agreement and then said respectfully, "Where might I find the blacksmith's shop, sir?"

"Just follow your nose," the fellow said, pointing as he headed down a side street, "and you can't miss it."

Phillip stirred John's old nag into action once more, and guided the horse and cart down the street. In just a minute or so, a sign hanging from the building at the end of the road caught his eye. *Michael Martin,* it said. *Bright-smith.*

Grinning, Phillip recalled the time he'd mistakenly called Geoffrey's father a blacksmith to his face. *Everyone* called the man a blacksmith, and Mr. Martin had more or less learned to live with the title. But those closest to him—those who ought to know better—got a lecture if they dared diminish his life's work.

"A blacksmith's work is plain and simple," he'd say, pointing a thick, greasy finger at them. "He's satisfied with things just as they come from his forge." He'd stand taller, tuck in his chin, and say, "Now a bright-smith. . .a bright-smith will polish the metal he manufactures to a considerable degree of nicety."

Nodding, he'd put down his hammer to make the final point: "Here's the way to tell the difference, boys. The blacksmith can *make* a bell, but it takes a bright-smith to shine it up and make it ring!"

As he braked the big cart, Phillip could hear each tinny *ping* of Mr. Martin's mallet as it bounced off the anvil. He tethered the horse to a hitching post and entered the smithy's shop.

"Excuse me, sir," he said, deliberately deepening his voice to disguise himself, "but I wonder. Can you tell me the difference between a blacksmith and a bright-smith?"

Without looking up from his work, Michael Martin said in a gruff voice, "It's like the difference between the Mystic River and the Atlantic Ocean. They'll both get you good and wet, but only one'll make you yearn to be at sea."

Mr Martin turned from the anvil and smiled. "Well, if it isn't young Phillip Smythe come to town! Thought you could fool me, did you now? What brings you here, m'boy?" Wiping his blackened hands on his grimy apron, he walked toward Phillip.

Using his thumb as a pointer, Phillip indicated the cart, visible beyond his shoulder. "I've brought you a load of pig iron."

The man's eyes lit up. "Why, you may as well have said you're delivering a wagonload of gold! Let's see it!"

Phillip led him outside and threw back the tarp to allow Mr. Martin to inspect the metal.

The smith lifted an ingot and turned it round and round in his big leathery hands. "Right hefty," he said. "I'll admit it's started me drooling, but I'm afraid I haven't the funds right now to pay you for it."

Phillip reached into his shirt pocket to withdraw a carefully folded packet of parchment. "I've sketched it all out for you," he said, handing the package to Mr. Martin.

The smithy gave the drawings a cursory inspection. "Why, these are the work-a-day tools of a carpenter. I've made

111

hundreds of 'em." Again he scrutinized Phillip. "Surely your father has a few like these to spare you as you apprentice."

"The tools aren't for me, sir," Phillip said. "A cyclone blew through Boston, you see, and what the winds didn't destroy, the floodwaters did." He hesitated, wondering whether or not to tell the man more. "It took nearly a hundred lives—George Sprague included. Flattened much of the town, including my father's workshop. We dug around in the rubble for days, but found just one tool."

Mr. Martin shook his head. "I'd heard something of the storm in Boston, but I'd no idea that it had cost George his life. That's a sad tale, for sure," he said, frowning. Then he brightened a bit and said, "I don't imagine there's a smithy in Boston who could take my place. And *that's* why your father sent you to have me make him some new tools. Am I right?"

"The truth is, my father has no idea I'm here. He's in London, you see, at the request of the governor. We're doing this—John and I, that is—so that when he returns, his shop and his tools will be just as he left them."

Mr. Martin grinned. "You always were a good and thoughtful boy, Phillip Smythe." He took a closer look at the drawings. "You'll affix handles to 'em, then, once I've made you the business end of the tools?"

Phillip nodded. "Yes, sir."

Suddenly, the man's brow furrowed. "Where'd you come by this iron, if you don't mind my asking?"

"Don't mind at all," he answered, grinning. "Do you remember the cave where Geoffrey and I saw the Indian?"

Chuckling, Mr. Martin said, "The one where the painted Pequot warrior nearly abducted the two of you, you mean?"

Phillip laughed. "Turns out he wasn't a Pequot after all, but a peaceful Narragansett. His name is White Wolf. Over time, we became friends. It was as he and I were getting acquainted that I noticed streaks of reddish-brown in the cave walls."

"How'd you know what it was?"

Phillip nodded. "White Wolf told me." He shrugged. "Of course, at first it meant nothing to me. But once I realized what it was. . ."

The excitement he felt raised his voice a level in tone and volume as he continued. "It took months to dig out enough of it to begin smelting. I used the only tool that wasn't washed away in the flood. . .a chisel." Grinning, he waited to see if Mr. Martin would get the joke.

"Not the same chisel you were going to use to carve off the nose of the Pequot!"

Flushing, Phillip grinned. "The very same."

Mr. Martin crossed one arm over his chest and rested his chin in a cupped palm. "Now let me get this straight. You're telling me you mined the ore and then smelted it, all by yourself. Why that would require more than a few measly tools, it would demand that you—"

"Build a furnace. And make smelting pots. Yes, I know." Phillip told him all about how he'd made the brick to construct the oven and about the way he'd lined wooden bowls and troughs and skimmers with clay to enable them to withstand the incredible heat of the melted iron.

"But where'd you learn it all, boy!"

"Why, from you, sir."

It was Mr. Martin's turn to blush. "Well, if I'd had any idea you were watching so closely, I'd have charged for my tutelage!" he said, laughing. "Now let me take a closer look at this pig iron you've brought all the way from a dark cave in Boston. If it's any good at all, I'll be more than glad to trade it for my smithy's services."

"What's Geoffrey up to these days?" Phillip asked, changing the subject as Mr. Martin examined the ingots.

"He's apprenticing to become a teacher. I'm sure you remember how my boy loved books. Well, one day he just walked right up to me, carefree as you please, and said, 'Father, I want to be a teacher, like Mr. Williams.' "

"But I always thought he'd follow in your footsteps."

"Well, that was *my* plan," Mr. Martin said, "but Geoffrey had other plans." He chuckled good-naturedly. "Just between you and me, he's far better with the books and the chalk than he ever could be with the forge and the bellows!"

Phillip stood stewing over this fact as his friend's father rummaged through the wagon, inspecting the chunks of iron.

"This is excellent, Phillip," Mr. Martin said, tumbling an ingot round and round in his big, leathery hands. "Simply excellent! It'll fire up and make fine, strong tools. You'll see. Why, I can hardly wait to get it to blood-red heat level and see how well it responds to the hammer. I'll wager it'll smooth right out like the back of a rich lady's hand!"

"How long do you think it'll take to get all the tools on the blueprints completed?"

"Well, I have a job ahead of yours." He replaced the ingot, then scrubbed his bristly chin with one gritty hand. "I suppose I can get to 'em day after tomorrow. It shouldn't take more than a week to finish up."

"I wonder if you could tell me where I might find the nearest hotel. Perhaps you know the owner, and could help me talk him into letting me work off some of my bed and board?"

Mr. Martin's laughter echoed up and down the street. "A hotel? In Salem? Surely you're joking. There's nothing like that in this town, m'boy. At least not yet! You'll stay at our house, of course, and I'll not hear another word about it."

He stepped onto the porch of his shop. "Now, why not drive this poor cart 'round back and let that old nag of yours have a good long drink of water while we unload the iron. Then you can head over to tell Mrs. Martin there'll be another plate to fill at supper tonight."

He clamped a fatherly hand onto Phillip's shoulder. "I wish I could see her face when she gets a look at who's come to town. She'll tie her apron in knots, I'll wager!"

Phillip did as he was told, his mind brewing with resentment as he unharnessed the horse, gave her a good brushing, and stood her at the water trough behind the smithy's shop. *Why can Jake and John and Geoffrey see their dreams come true,* he demanded of no one, *yet I cannot!* When the mare had had her fill, Phillip led her into the stall with Mr. Martin's horses.

"Off with you, now!" the smithy insisted once they'd unloaded the iron. "And when you see that wife of mine, tell her for me that my stomach has been growling for a batch of her corn bread all the livelong day! You'll find her two streets over, first house on the right," he instructed. "Don't forget, now," he concluded, patting his ample belly, "fresh-baked corn bread!"

Phillip forced himself to smile, then headed for the Martins's house. What would he say when Geoffrey finally returned from his day of apprenticing with Roger Williams? One thing was certain: *I'd best get hold of my envy before it gets the best of me. It isn't Geoffrey's fault that things worked out in his favor.*

He would do the right thing. When he saw his old friend, he'd grab his pudgy hand and pump the pudgy arm up and down. "Congratulations!" he'd say. "I'm so happy for you!"

It was true after all. He *did* believe that his friend deserved hearty well-wishes, and he *was* happy that the boy had found a way to make a living at the career of his choice.

Yes, he would do the right thing.

Didn't he *always?*

CHAPTER THIRTEEN
Geoffrey's Lesson

Phillip would have known Geoffrey anywhere, despite the fact that he'd grown a foot taller. The soft belly that had always hung over his belt of his breeches was gone now, replaced by firm, muscled flesh. His hair had darkened a bit to a shade more coppery than carroty. He wore a starched linen shirt beneath his leather jerkin and doublet, and a crowned hat with a wide brim that shaded his face, making it impossible for Phillip to see whether or not his freckles were still in full bloom.

He looked into his friend's wide blue eyes and smiled. "It's good to see you again, Geoffrey," he admitted.

The boy removed his hat and held out his right hand. "Good to see you, too."

Indeed, the freckles had all but disappeared. Geoffrey was no longer the boy Phillip remembered. He, too, was becoming a man.

"I hear you're apprenticing with Mr. Williams," he said, shaking the outstretched hand. "Well, good for you."

"Not with Mr. Williams," Geoffrey corrected, "but do you know where this practice originated?" He pointed with his left hand to the hands the friends had clasped in friendly greeting.

Phillip grinned and rolled his eyes. "No, but I'm sure you're about to tell me." *At least that hasn't changed,* Phillip told himself.

"In the olden days, when men wore armor everywhere they went and carried spears and cutlasses, they often didn't know when they'd encounter an enemy on the road. So they carried sharp knives to protect themselves from surprise attacks."

Geoffrey let go of Phillip's hand and positioned himself as one might on the battlefield. "Extending the hand, you see, was the way to show a man you were unarmed—or at the very least, that you had no intention of inflicting harm."

Phillip could only smile and shake his head. "You will be a fine teacher, Geoffrey. Your students will sit silent all the day long, with their eyes glued to you!"

Geoffrey's grin threatened to split his face in two. "Do you think so, Phillip? Do you really think I'll make a good teacher?"

"I do," he said and meant it. "It's what you were born to do." As the boys began walking toward the Martins's house, Phillip slung an arm over his friend's shoulders. "Remember the way you used to give me lessons in grammar and history and literature as we played?"

"Do I!" Geoffrey exclaimed. "And I remember that you weren't overly fond of the instruction, too!"

Phillip removed his arm from Geoffrey's shoulder. "Oh, I put on a good show for you, but I didn't mind, really. In fact," he said, playfully poking an elbow into his friend's side, "I rather enjoyed it. I believe your teachings and my good grades in Mr. Williams's class were directly related!"

Geoffrey laughed. "So tell me, what brings you to Salem?" Suddenly, he stopped, stood in Phillip's path, and placed both hands on his friend's shoulders. "Wait. Don't tell me. Your family has decided to live here, too!"

He shook his head. "I'm afraid not. I'm here to trade with your father."

Phillip proceeded to fill Geoffrey in on the events leading up to his appearance in Salem, from the storm that destroyed Boston to the death of his sister. "I'll be here a week or so— just long enough to have those tools made."

Geoffrey pocketed both hands as the boys resumed walking. "I'm sorry to hear about Sarah. How's Jake taking it?"

"He didn't do so well at first. It was months before his eyes weren't red-rimmed. But he held it together, saying he was doing it for his baby daughter." Phillip shrugged. "Whatever the reason, it was good to have him back."

"And little Leah? How's she these days?"

Phillip smiled. "You'd hardly recognize her, Geoff. She's grown taller, and there's actually meat on her little bird-bones! Her cheeks are pink and her hair shines—all because of Jake's concoctions!"

Geoffrey nodded. "That's good to hear," he said, grinning. "She deserves a happy, healthy life. It must make Jake feel good, knowing what a positive influence he's having on people's lives. I declare, if I didn't believe God put me on the earth to be a teacher, I'd become an apothecary. It's fascinating work, and Leah's proof of all the good it does. Who wouldn't be proud of such a life choice?"

Anyone would be proud to call himself an apothecary, Phillip said to himself. He took a deep breath. This was neither the time nor the place for self-pity. "So tell me, how's our Roger Williams? Has he been arrested?"

Geoffrey laughed at that. "He came a hair's breadth from being expelled from the colony, but he escaped. He's with the Narragansetts, and there's talk that he'll be leaving in the spring for places farther north. We'll be going with him if he moves to help him develop a new settlement."

"I'm sorry to hear that," Phillip said, frowning. "When your father told me you were apprenticing to become a teacher, I naturally assumed he was your teacher. I had no idea he'd

120

been forced to flee again."

Geoffrey nodded. "Yes. It's sad, isn't it? They would have sent him back to England if they'd caught him." He rolled his eyes and sighed. "God only knows what his fate might have been if that had happened." Wiggling his eyebrows and smirking, he added, "The man has a talent for stirring up a vat of trouble. Why, I hear he's putting together some kind of deal with the Indians to buy land for his followers."

Mr. Williams, Phillip recalled, had always been a staunch advocate of the natives, believing it was his Christian duty to treat them fairly, for they were every bit as loved by God as anyone who had crossed the Atlantic to come to this land. It was just like him to create a town where men would be free to follow the dictates of their hearts in matters of religion *and* politics.

He remembered one of Williams's particularly strong lectures: "We were allowed to come here only to make a profit for the Crown; but the colonies, as commercial ventures, will be written down in history as utter failures. Success will come to those who yearn—and fight—for freedom!"

"So who *are* you apprenticing with, if not Roger Williams?"

"Pastor Cummings. He's not all fire and brimstone, like Mr. Williams, but I think his quiet, gentle way reaches more ears. No offense to Mr. Williams, understand, but I believe I'll follow the Cummings approach to teaching and leave the hollering to those with the voices and the temperaments for it!"

Phillip couldn't help but agree. Geoffrey's soft-spoken ways would coax information *into* his students and would coax

121

interest in their subjects *out* of them.

"Enough about me and Roger Williams," Geoffrey said. "What about you? How's your work with Jake going?"

Phillip clenched his teeth and hid his tight-fisted hands in his pockets. "I'm not working with Jake."

"Well, why on earth not? You're the perfect type to be an apothecary!"

"Between working on the college, keeping up with chores around the house, and getting things ready to visit your father, there's barely been time for eating and sleeping. It's obvious I wasn't intended to be an apothecary. I'll be a carpenter, like my father, and his father before him, and his father before that."

He shrugged. "Guess it's only fitting and proper, since I seem to be fairly handy with the tools of the trade."

Geoffrey was silent for a long time. "Have you completely given up hope, then?"

"Of being an apothecary, you mean?"

The redhead nodded.

Phillip didn't even realize that, as he answered, his shoulders slumped. "Yes. I guess you'd have to say I've given up all hope."

"Then you're a fool, Phillip. I believe it's what God intended for you." He stopped walking, faced his friend, and placed a hand on his shoulder. "No one could argue that you've had a hard time, or that life hasn't been difficult these past months. But exercise a little patience, why don't you? I'd wager you'll find this has all been a temporary setback."

He pocketed the hand that had rested on Phillip's shoulder. "If you don't have faith, what have you *got?*"

Phillip's brow furrowed. "Make no mistake, Geoffrey. I have faith in the one person who has never let me down: *myself.*"

After their serious discussion about faith, Phillip and Geoffrey hadn't been able to pick up their former good-natured attitudes. All in all, though, it had been a good week.

Phillip had worked in the shop with Mr. Martin, helping to re-create the tools his father had lost in the flood. When he returned from London, Father would have a ready supply of saws, planes, hammers, awls, chisels, and gimlets. He'd have only the best pincers, and a turkey-stone on which to sharpen them all.

Phillip watched with avid interest as with hammer and tong each glowing implement slowly took shape. Steam rose to the smoky ceiling of the forge as Mr. Martin quenched each heated piece from cherry red to shining ebony.

He'd bring them home, wrapped in a leather scarf, and lay them out on the workbench John had already built. His brother had built a sturdy stool, too, and a long-handled toolbox in which their father could carry his equipment to and from the shop.

When Phillip returned from Salem, they spent their evenings reconstructing the workshop from boards they'd scavenged from town. Mr. Martin, hearing all the brothers had planned for their father, had contributed a wagonload of lumber and a bucket of nails.

"It's the least I can do," he insisted, "since I got far more than a few tools' worth of iron out of you." Shaking a stubby finger at Phillip, he'd added, "I'll not have 'em saying in Boston that Michael Martin would cheat a boy!"

Folks in town retired by nine o'clock in the evening. To keep from waking their neighbors, Phillip and John were forced to lay down their tools at that hour. But all was not lost. Between nine and midnight, the brothers worked quietly in Cousin Catherine's kitchen, boiling the skins of all kinds of beasts to produce a jelly from which they made glue. The older the animal, they discovered, the better the glue.

Slowly, board by board, nail by nail, the workshop took form. And what a workshop it was at twenty feet across the front, and forty feet deep. Their father had never been an ordinary carpenter. Many spoke of his cabinetry skills. Those talents had inspired the governor to send him to England. And many a housewife had drooled over his lovely chairs and his intricately carved, highly polished tables and bureaus.

So Phillip and John decided to build Father's workshop two stories high, to enable him to work on more than one project at a time. Downstairs, he might put together a set of fir rafters while upstairs, the close-doored space protected the varnish of a curio cabinet from the effects of the sawdust that floated freely and frequently in his shop.

One night over supper, Hannah announced that in the summer, there would be another hungry mouth to feed. "A son perhaps," she said, lovingly stroking her belly, "to carry on the Smythe name for yet another generation."

John could not have been more pleased. "Children are what it's all about," he declared, wrapping her in a hearty hug that lifted her clean off her feet. "What we're building here has no purpose if there's no one to carry it on when we're gone!"

Jake, who took most of his evening meals with the family, gathered little Hope in his arms. "Congratulations," he said quietly. "It's good to see life going on."

Phillip followed him into the dimming daylight. "Let me walk with you to your house," he said, falling into step beside his brother-in-law. "It's been so long since we've had a chance to talk."

"That it has," the Irishman said. "That it has."

"Do you ever miss Ireland, Jake?"

"Aye, I miss her a lot. 'Specially lately."

"Why lately?"

"Because," he said, switching Hope to his other hip, "I'd promised Sarah we'd go there someday. Not to stay, mind you, but so I could show her where her daughter's roots were planted." His voice took on an extra lilt, reminding Phillip of days long past when the very sight of Sarah would put a smile on Jake's face that could light up an entire room. "Ah, she'd have loved it there, all bright and green and grassy."

He grew quiet and lowered his head.

"I miss her, too," Phillip said, understanding the reason behind Jake's sudden silence. "Sometimes, I ask God why He didn't take me instead."

Jake frowned. "I'll hear no more of your foolish talk. Sarah's gone, and that's that. Sure, we all miss her. She was the light of our lives. God doesn't make deals, Phillip."

"But *why* did He take Sarah? She was so sweet, so gentle."

"There are questions in life that'll never be answered, Phil, and that, I'm afraid, is one of 'em. 'For who hath known the mind of the Lord? or who hath been his counsellor?' "

"Well, quoting Romans doesn't heal the pain of her loss."

"Aye, you've got that right. But it heals the lack of faith."

Phillip met Jake's eyes and saw that his sister's husband understood the doubts and fears that had been plaguing him.

"You'll know the answers, Phillip, when you join her." He gave the boy a playful nudge. "Are you in a hurry to meet your Maker?"

He couldn't help but grin. "No, I don't suppose I am."

"Well, then, be happy for John and Hannah. And for little Zach, too, for now he'll have a young sibling to bully! I'm not sayin' you should forget your sister. God knows that'd be impossible for me! All I'm sayin' is, let it be. It weren't nobody's fault, so stop torturing yourself by trying to lay blame."

It was good advice, and Phillip knew it, felt it, deep in his soul. They were standing at the gate now, where Sarah had so often stood to hand Phillip a treat for his lunch as he walked to work. He would take Jake's advice and remember her that way, smiling and happy, fit and healthy.

"How's the shop these days, Jake?"

He pushed open the gate and latched it behind him without inviting Phillip inside. "It's fine. Every jar and bottle full to the brim. Now get on with you," he said, winking. "Looks like rain tonight. Why not take a break and get yourself some much-needed rest?"

Phillip took a deep breath. "I might just do that. There's very little to do."

"By the way, I heard in town today they spotted a ship on the horizon."

Phillip's heart hammered, and his palms grew damp, despite the chill breeze. "Heading north or south?"

"Oh, she set sail in London, to be sure," Jake said. "And I'll be mighty surprised if your father isn't on her."

"What's your guess? Will she drop anchor in a day or two? A week?"

Jake squinted up at the darkening sky. "If the weather holds, I believe we'll be gathering for a welcome dinner this time next week. Now get yourself home, before those thunderheads open up and drench you good!"

Phillip gazed up at the thick clouds, too. "G'night, Jake. Sleep tight, Hope," he called over his shoulder as he headed home.

Who can know the mind of God? Jake had quoted. "I pray it's in Your mind to bring my father home, safe and sound," Phillip whispered.

But Jake's last words reverberated in his mind: *If the weather holds. . .if the weather holds. . .if the weather holds. . .*

CHAPTER FOURTEEN
Dreams Fulfilled

The entire family had gathered at the harbor, waiting for the landing boat that would hopefully be carrying Father back to Boston. Phillip squinted hard at the passengers on the float, trying to pick out his father's face.

"Father! It's Father!" Leah cried out.

And then he saw the familiar hat, and the same doublet he'd been wearing when he left town.

Phillip could recite, at any given time, precisely how long it had been since he'd watched his father's form growing smaller, smaller, as he headed for the harbor. As of today, he'd been away for twenty months, one week, two and one-half days.

He'd arrive with a pocketful of coins and a head full of stories to tell about his time in the king's castle, no doubt. But all that could wait.

"John," Phillip whispered, elbowing his older brother, "how long must we wait to show him the workshop?"

John smiled a bit. "Well, I think we ought to give him a chance to hug Mother, at least. What do you think?"

"I suppose," he said. "And after he dispenses a round of hugs and kisses, *then* can we show him the workshop?"

"Let's give him time to believe he has months of hard work ahead of him. He'll have a hearty meal, and catch up on town gossip, and listen to all the bad news. . . ."

John grew silent so suddenly, it made Phillip look away from the boat for the first time since he'd spotted his father on board it. A quick study of his brother's face told him John didn't relish facing his father with what he'd done in the man's absence.

"He needs to hear the details about Sarah's death, of course, but I don't think it's really necessary to tell him *everything* right away." Sooner or later, of course, Father would find out about the gambling, the grog, and the resulting fire. "At least, not right away."

John ruffled his younger brother's hair. "Let him feel good

and grateful for the little bit of work I contributed to the workshop, eh, before drawing him a picture of what a lout I am."

"You are not now, nor were you ever, a lout." Phillip returned his gaze to the ferry. "You got a mite off track, is all. You found your way back quick enough. That's the important thing."

"He's going to be very proud of you," John said. "You held this family together. I don't know what would have become of us, if not for you."

"Be quiet, John," Leah whispered. "I think I hear Father calling to us."

The two brothers followed Leah's gaze toward the ferry, where the man nearest the rail slowly waved his hat back and forth. "What's he saying?" John asked. "I can't make it out."

" 'Home at last!' he's saying, 'Home at last!' " Leah shouted.

Just as John had predicted, the greeting began with a flurry of hugs and kisses and well-wishes. Father couldn't get over how well Leah looked, but it was clear that he missed being greeted by Sarah as well. They told him about the fire as they walked toward Catherine's house.

Father took his cousin's hand in his. "You were mighty generous to open your home to us."

"What's mine is yours and always shall be," was all she said. But when at last they arrived at her house, she ushered Father and Mother inside and shooed the rest of the family down the walk.

"We'll leave them alone for a little while, so that William can take a nap and Abigail can fix him a cup of tea." Over her shoulder, she called to Father and Mother, "We'll be down the road at Jake's house if you need anything."

When Father and Mother arrived at Jake's house several hours later, their eyes and faces were swollen, and it was apparent by their stuffy noses that both had been crying.

Mother has told him about John, Phillip said to himself, *and filled him in on the details of Sarah's death. The doctor had taken it upon himself to post a letter on the very day we lost her, of course, but surely he hadn't described the particulars.*

Mother brought with her a huge pot of steaming stew, and Father carried a napkin-covered basket filled with flaky biscuits and mint jelly. *How like Mother to keep her hands busy as she said what needed saying,* Phillip decided.

There was just enough time before supper for a short walk. "Let's head for town," Phillip suggested. "You won't believe what a good job they did repairing the church," he added, knowing full well that to get to the heart of the city, they'd have to pass the site of Father's former workshop.

Mother, knowing what her boys were up to, lifted a toddling Hope from the floor and stuffed her into her surprised grandfather's arms. The child managed to distract the man, tugging at his ears and sticking wet kisses to his cheeks and lips. But nothing the little girl did could keep his attention from the site of his former workshop.

Instead of the bare ground he expected to see, Father was

confronted with a brand-new workshop, bigger and better than the old one.

"Your mother told me you boys had done something wonderful. But I never expected *this*."

He stepped over the threshold and into the dim space. Closing his eyes, he tilted back his head and took a deep breath of air. "There's no perfume as sweet as the scent of fresh-cut wood."

"That's because wood's in your blood," Jake said, grinning. "Take note of what's up those stairs, there, why don't you?" he suggested to his father-in-law.

Still balancing Hope on his hip, Father climbed the staircase. His heavy footfalls echoed above Phillip, John, Leah, and Jake as they waited in the main workspace.

The footsteps halted, and there was such a stillness in the place that Phillip wondered if the others gathered near could hear the furious hammering of his heart.

When Father returned to them at last, he handed Hope to Jake and examined the shop. Suddenly, he noticed the tools lying neatly on the smooth-sanded surface of the workbench. Lifting an awl, he turned it round and round in his hands. "Where did it come from?"

"Phillip mined the ore from that old cave near the Mystic River," Jake began. "Then he melted it down and took the ingots up to Michael Martin in Salem. Martin forged the ore, and Phillip made the handles."

Father's gaze locked on his son. "You did all this and built a college as well?"

Phillip felt his cheeks flush. "Well, I didn't build Harvard single-handedly."

"But you did this alone," Father said, knowingly. He put the tool back where he'd found it. "And I thought I had the greater gift to give," he said softly.

Phillip's brow furrowed with confusion. "I don't underst—"

"You will, soon enough," Father interrupted. Jutting out his chin, he said, "We'd best be getting back before the women send out a search party." Patting his lean stomach, he added, "I haven't had a decent, home-cooked meal in a long, long time."

Throughout the meal, Phillip puzzled over the remark his father had made: "And I thought I had the greater gift to give." Finally, the boy decided to enjoy the stew. *Father will provide the riddle's answer when it's time,* he told himself.

After supper, Father settled into the big wooden rocker near the hearth. He had brought each of them a small gift, which he'd stuffed into his satchel. Balancing it on his lap, he began handing out the treasures.

"First, here's something for the love of my life," he said, pulling a small black velvet box from the sack.

Mother took it in trembling hands and sat beside him on the hearth. The lid creaked quietly when she opened it. For a moment, she could only stare wide-eyed at the container's contents. "Oh, William. It's lovely. So very lovely."

She removed the brooch from its bed of white satin and held it aloft to catch the waning light from the window beside the fireplace. Her gaze met his, but only for a moment, and in that

133

tick in time, all gathered could read the love written there.

Mother pinned the brooch to the knot of her shawl. "Such an extravagant gift!" she exclaimed. "Why, I'll be the envy of every lady in Boston!"

Father leaned forward to accept her kiss. "You were the envy of every lady in Boston the day we arrived here, my love." He continued to look into her eyes for a moment, then pulled back, as if suddenly aware of his audience.

"Well, now," he said. "There are many more surprises in my bag of tricks. Who will be next?"

He began by giving baby Hope some hand-carved blocks. Then he turned to Leah and presented her with a rectangular box. "I am proud of what a thoughtful young lady you have grown to be while I was gone," he said. "Your mother has told me how you have used the gift of your good health to help your brothers and Hope. I am blessed to call you daughter."

Leah hid her blushes by giving Father a big hug. Then she opened the mysterious package. Inside was the most beautiful doll she had ever seen. It was dressed in an exact replica of a court lady's dress. "Oh, Father," she exclaimed. "I've never seen a doll as nice as this."

Father glowed with pleasure. "She may be beautiful," he said, "but her external beauty doesn't hold a candle to the lovely spirit I see in my daughter."

Next Father gave gifts to John and his family, to Jake, and to Cousin Catherine and Thomas, thanking them all for their part in keeping the family together during his absence.

At last, he turned to Phillip. "I'm afraid yours is the only gift that doesn't come in a package," Father said. "In fact, the only thing I can show you is a slip of paper."

Phillip's heart beat hard with anticipation. What could this paper his father was taking from the battered leather valise mean?

He met his father's eyes. "Your mother told me everything," Father said. "I'm giving this to you now because it's time. You've earned it. You carried quite a load while I was away, and for the most part, carried it alone. And your mother says you did it all without a word of complaint."

Father paused and handed Phillip a sealed note. "Go ahead, Phillip," he said, his eyes twinkling. "Read it. Read it aloud so everyone can hear it."

With shaky hands, Phillip broke the seal on the paper and unfolded it. Speaking slowly, to try to control the tremor in his voice, he began reading:

"To my dear son, Phillip,

"After more than a year of putting aside your own desires to meet the needs of others, it is time for you to follow your dreams. I have arranged with my son-in-law Jake for you to become an apprentice apothecary. . . ."

Phillip's voice trailed off. Leah's cheers seemed far away, and Jake's knowing grin couldn't quite come into focus. Was it possible? He'd thought his dreams were dead. How could this be? Suddenly Father's voice broke through the haze that had surrounded Phillip.

"I had plenty of time to think on it, Phillip," Father explained. "You have every right to do with your life what you feel the

Lord has called you to do. If an apothecary is your calling, so be it."

"You mean. . ." He shook the letter in his hand. "You mean you planned to give me this gift, even before you knew?"

"Before I knew all you'd done on my behalf? Yes. Even before that. And now that I *do* know, I'm more determined than ever to see you live out your dream."

"But. . .but. . ."

Father's raised hand silenced his son. "I know you thought your dreams were dead. But remember God's words recorded in the book of Jeremiah: 'For I know the thoughts that I think toward you, saith the Lord, thoughts of peace, and not of evil, to give you an expected end.' "

Phillip looked at his father with puzzled eyes.

"You see," Father explained, "sometimes life is difficult, and it is easy to wonder if God enjoys seeing us suffer. But He doesn't. He wants to bring peace and hope to our lives—an end we can look forward to with expectancy."

He reached out, took Mother's hand, and pulled her into a warm embrace. "I can't imagine being happier than I am right this minute," he admitted, "right here, surrounded by my loved ones. But I am still saddened, because as much as I find myself looking for Sarah and George, they are not with us.

"Yet even in our sadness, God has given us something to look forward to. One day we will all be reunited with them in heaven. Because of Jesus' death for us, we can look to the future with hope."

Phillip's face lit up with a smile of understanding. God did love him. No matter how dark things might seem in the future, he would remember that God was working to bring peace and hope to his life.

The family members pressed close, chattering and giggling and congratulating Phillip on his apprenticeship. Amid the happy din, Phillip stood, holding the paper that promised so much.

Phillip had traveled from Plymouth to Boston, from Boston to Salem, from Salem back to Boston—little trips, he knew, in comparison to the one he was about to take.

Soon, he would embark on a journey like none he'd experienced to date. Soon, he'd begin a journey toward capturing his dream.

Good News for Readers

There's more!

As *Queen Anne's War* begins, warships have entered Boston Harbor. At first Will and Beth Smith are excited to see all the soldiers landing in Boston Harbor. But that's before their brother-in-law Rob leaves with the troops that will head north to fight the French.

Waiting to find out if Rob is still alive, Will and Beth face their own problems. Pranks at school are endangering some of the younger students, and everyone thinks Will is to blame. They know that Jeremy Clark is really behind the trouble, but how will they get anyone to believe them?

Your Child Is In for the Ultimate American Adventure!

A new book series and fun club for 8 to 12 year-olds! Told through the eyes of kids like yours, *The American Adventure* books will immerse your boy or girl in the action of key events from the *Mayflower* to WWII. Your child will learn America's story and clearly see God's hand throughout our nation's history.

Famous and not-so-famous personalities that have shaped our nation will become living, breathing people. Your child will see how a person's strength of character and depth of conviction influence decisions that impact people, nations, and even the entire world—for hundreds of years.

These kinds of lessons aren't easily learned from typical history books. But in *The American Adventure* books, the lessons are clear, compelling, and unforgettable.

Your first FREE book, *The Mayflower Adventure*, tells of persecution, peril on the ocean, and the excitement of a new land. Mail this coupon today to receive FREE *The Mayflower Adventure*, along with the trial book, *Plymouth Pioneers*. You pay only $3.99 if you choose to keep *Plymouth Pioneers*, or you may return it within 15 days and owe nothing. When you pay for the trial book, your child will be enrolled as a Charter Member of *The American Adventure Club* (includes Member Card, Poster, Stickers, Activity Book, Newsletter, and more) and will receive two new books every month for only $7.98.

You may return any book you're not satisfied with within 15 days and pay nothing, and you may cancel your membership anytime. Whatever you decide, *The Mayflower Adventure* is yours to keep. Your child will love it, so act now!

❏ **YES**, send me *FREE* The Mayflower Adventure, and the trial book!

Child's Name_____ Age_____

Parent's Name_____

Address_____

City_____ State_____ Zip_____

Parent Initial Here_____   Adpg98

Mail to: American Adventure Book Club, PO Box 722, Uhrichsville, OH 44683-0722